CHARMED LIFE

Gwendolen Chant was obviously
destined for Great Things. The cards
said she was going to rule the world,
though Cat, her brother, didn't see
how that was possible. But everyone
in Coven Street believed in
Gwendolen's future, including Mr
Nostrum who was tutoring her in
witchcraft. So no one was surprised
when the elegant stranger appeared,
and the two young Chants were
translated from seedy Coven Street
to the grandeur of Chrestomanci
Castle. It was very luxurious and
pleasant at the Castle and Cat would
have enjoyed it thoroughly if he
hadn't been so terrified by
Chrestomanci himself. Who was
Chrestomanci? And why were they
there? *Winner of the 1978 Guardian
Children's Fiction Award.*

CHARMED LIFE

Diana Wynne Jones

A Lythway Book

CHIVERS PRESS
BATH

First published 1977
by
Macmillan Children's Books
This Large Print edition published by
Chivers Press
by arrangement with the author
and in the U.S.A. with
William Morrow & Company, Inc
1987

ISBN 0 7451 0490 8

British Library Cataloguing in Publication Data

Jones, Diana Wynne
    Charmed life.—Large print ed.—
    (A Lythway book)
    I. Title
    823'.914[J]   PZ7

    ISBN 0–7451–0490–8

For Claire, Nicholas and Frances

CHARMED LIFE

CHAPTER ONE

Cat Chant admired his elder sister Gwendolen. She was a witch. He admired her and he clung to her. Great changes came about in their lives and left him no one else to cling to.

The first great change came about when their parents took them out for a day trip down the river in a paddle steamer. They set out in great style, Gwendolen and her mother in white dresses with ribbons, Cat and his father in prickly blue serge Sunday suits. It was a hot day. The steamer was crammed with other people in holiday clothes, talking, laughing, eating whelks with thin slices of white bread and butter, while the paddleboat steam organ wheezed out popular tunes so that no one could hear themselves talk.

In fact the steamer was too crowded and too old. Something went wrong with the steering. The whole laughing, whelk-eating, Sunday-dressed crowd was swept away in the current from the

1

weir. They hit one of the posts which were supposed to stop people being swept away, and the paddle steamer, being old, simply broke into pieces. Cat remembered the organ playing and the paddles beating the blue sky. Clouds of steam screamed from broken pipes and drowned the screams from the crowd, as every single person aboard was swept away through the weir. It was a terrible accident. The papers called it the Saucy Nancy Disaster. The ladies in their clinging skirts were quite unable to swim. The men in tight blue serge were very little better off. But Gwendolen was a witch, so she could not drown. And Cat, who flung his arms round Gwendolen when the boat hit the post, survived too. There were very few other survivors.

The whole country was shocked by it. The paddleboat company and the town of Wolvercote between them paid for the funerals. Gwendolen and Cat were given heavy black clothes at public expense, and rode behind the procession of hearses in a carriage pulled by black horses with black plumes on their heads.

The other survivors rode with them. Cat looked at them and wondered if they were witches and warlocks, but he never found out. The Mayor of Wolvercote had set up a Fund for the survivors. Money poured in from all over the country. All the other survivors took their share and went away to start new lives elsewhere. Only Cat and Gwendolen were left and, since nobody could discover any of their relations, they stayed in Wolvercote.

They became celebrities for a time. Everyone was very kind. Everyone said what beautiful little orphans they were. It was true. They were both fair and pale, with blue eyes, and looked good in black. Gwendolen was very pretty, and tall for her age. Cat was small for his age. Gwendolen was very motherly to Cat, and people were touched. Cat did not mind. It made up a little for the empty, lost way he was feeling. Ladies gave him cake and toys. Town Councillors came and asked how he was getting on; and the Mayor called and patted him on the head. The Mayor explained that the money from the Fund was being put into a Trust for them until they were grown up. Meanwhile, the town would pay for their education and upbringing.

'And where would you little people like to live?' he asked kindly.

Gwendolen at once said that old Mrs Sharp downstairs had offered to take them in. 'She's been ever so kind to us,' she explained. 'We'd love to live with her.'

Mrs Sharp had been very kind. She was a witch too—the printed sign in her parlour window said *Certified Witch*—and interested in Gwendolen. The Mayor was a little dubious. Like all people who had no talent for witchcraft, he did not approve of those who had. He asked Cat how he felt about Gwendolen's plan. Cat did not mind. He preferred living in the house he was used to, even if it was downstairs. Since the Mayor felt that the two orphans ought to be made as happy as possible, he agreed. Gwendolen and Cat moved in with Mrs Sharp.

Looking back on it, Cat supposed that it was from this time on that he was certain Gwendolen was a witch. He had not been sure before. When he had asked his parents, they had shaken their heads, sighed, and looked unhappy. Cat had been puzzled, because he remembered the terrible trouble there had been when Gwendolen gave him cramps. He could not see how his parents could blame Gwendolen for it unless she truly was a witch. But all that was changed now. Mrs Sharp made no secret of it.

'You've a real talent for magic, dearie,' she said, beaming at Gwendolen, 'and I wouldn't be doing my duty by you if I let it go to waste. We must see about a teacher for you right away. You could do worse than go to Mr Nostrum next door for a start. He may be the worst necromancer in town, but he knows how to teach. He'll give you a good grounding, my love.'

Mr Nostrum's charges for teaching magic turned out to be £1 an hour for the Elementary Grades, and a guinea an hour for the Advanced Grades beyond. Rather expensive, as Mrs Sharp said. She put on her best hat with black beads and ran round to the Town Hall to see if the Fund would pay for Gwendolen's lessons.

To her annoyance, the Mayor refused. He told Mrs Sharp that witchcraft was not part of an ordinary education. Mrs Sharp came back rattling the beads on her hat with irritation, and carrying a flat cardboard box the Mayor had given her, full of the odds and ends the kind ladies had cleared out of Gwendolen's parents' bedroom.

'Blind prejudice!' Mrs Sharp said, dumping the box on the kitchen table. 'If a person has a gift, they have a right to have it developed—and so I told him! But don't worry, dearie,' she said, seeing that Gwendolen was looking decidedly stormy. 'There's a way round everything. Mr Nostrum would teach you for nothing, if we found the right thing to tempt him with. Let's have a look in this box. Your poor Ma and Pa may have left something that might be just the thing.'

Accordingly, Mrs Sharp turned the box out on to the table. It was a queer collection of things—letters and lace and souvenirs. Cat did not remember having seen half of them before. There was a marriage certificate, saying that Francis John Chant had married Caroline Mary Chant twelve years ago at St Margaret's Church, Wolvercote, and a withered nosegay his mother must have carried at the wedding. Underneath that, he found some glittery earrings he had never seen his mother wear.

Mrs Sharp's hat rattled as she bent swiftly over these. 'Those are diamond earrings!' she said. 'Your Ma must have had money! Now, if I took those to Mr Nostrum—But we'd get more for them if I took them round to Mr Larkins.' Mr Larkins kept the junk-shop on the corner of the street—except that it was not always exactly junk. Among the brass fenders and chipped crockery, you could find quite valuable things and also a discreet notice saying *Exotic Supplies*— which meant that Mr Larkins also stocked bats' wings, dried newts and other ingredients of magic. There was no question that Mr Larkins would be very interested in a pair of diamond earrings. Mrs Sharp's eyes pouched up, greedy and beady, as she put out her

7

hand to pick up the earrings.

Gwendolen put out her hand for them at the same moment. She did not say anything. Neither did Mrs Sharp. Both their hands stood still in the air. There was a feeling of fierce invisible struggle. Then Mrs Sharp took her hand away. 'Thank you,' Gwendolen said coldly, and put the earrings away in the pocket of her black dress.

'You see what I mean?' Mrs Sharp said, making the best of it. 'You have real talent, dearie!' She went back to sorting the other things in the box. She turned over an old pipe, ribbons, a spray of white heather, menus, concert tickets, and picked up a bundle of old letters. She ran her thumb down the edge of it. 'Love letters,' she said. 'His to her.' She put the bundle down without looking at it and picked up another. 'Hers to him. No use.' Cat, watching Mrs Sharp's broad mauve thumb whirring down a third bundle of letters, thought that being a witch must save a great deal of time. 'Business letters,' said Mrs Sharp. Her thumb paused, and went slowly back up the pile again.

'Now what have we here?' she said. She untied the pink tape round the bundle and carefully took out three letters. She unfolded them.

'Chrestomanci!' she exclaimed. And, as soon as she said it, she clapped one hand over her mouth and mumbled behind it. Her face was red. Cat could see she was surprised, frightened and greedy, all at the same time. 'Now what was *he* doing writing to your Pa?' she said, as soon as she had recovered.

'Let's see,' said Gwendolen.

Mrs Sharp spread the three letters out on the kitchen table, and Gwendolen and Cat bent over them. The first thing that struck Cat was the energy of the signature on all three:

The next thing he saw was that two of the letters were written in the same energetic writing as the signature. The first was dated twelve years ago, soon after his parents had been married. It said:

9

Dear Frank,
Now don't get on your high horse. I only offered because I thought it might help. I still will help, in any way I can, if you let me know what I can do. I feel you have a claim on me.

Yrs ever,
Chrestomanci

The second letter was shorter:

Dear Chant,
The same to you. Go to blazes.

Chrestomanci

The third letter was dated six years ago, and it was written by someone else. Chrestomanci had only signed it.

Sir,
You were warned six years ago that something like what you relate might come to pass, and you made it quite clear that you wished for no help from this quarter. We are not interested in your troubles. Nor is this a charitable institution.

Chrestomanci

10

'What did your Pa *say* to him?' Mrs Sharp wondered, curious and awestruck. 'Well—what do you think, dearie?'

Gwendolen held her hands spread out above the letters, rather as if she was warming them at a fire. Both her little fingers twitched. 'I don't know. They feel important—specially the first one and the last one—awfully important.'

'Who's Chrestomanci?' Cat asked. It was a hard name to say. He said it in pieces, trying to remember the way Mrs Sharp had said it: KREST-OH-MAN-SEE. 'Is that the right way?'

'Yes, that's right—and never you mind who he is, my love,' said Mrs Sharp. 'And important's a weak word for it, dearie. I wish I knew what your Pa had *said*. Something not many people'd dare say, by the sound of it. And look what he got in return! Three genuine signatures! Mr Nostrum would give his eyes for those, dearie. Oh, you're in luck! He'll teach you for those all right! So would any necromancer in the country.'

11

Gleefully, Mrs Sharp began packing the things away in the box again. 'What have we here?' A little red book of matches had fallen out of the bundle of business letters. Mrs Sharp took it up carefully and, quite as carefully, opened it. It was less than half full of flimsy cardboard matches. But three of the matches had been burnt, without being torn out of the book first. The third one along was so very burnt that Cat supposed it must have set light to the other two.

'Hm,' said Mrs Sharp. 'I think you'd better keep this, dearie.' She passed the little red book to Gwendolen, who put it in the pocket of her dress along with the earrings. 'And what about you having this, my love?' Mrs Sharp said to Cat, remembering that he had a claim too. She gave him the spray of white heather. Cat wore it in his button-hole until it fell to pieces.

Living with Mrs Sharp, Gwendolen seemed to expand. Her hair seemed brighter gold, her eyes deeper blue, and her whole manner was glad and confident. Perhaps Cat contracted a little to make room for her—he did not know. Not that he was unhappy. Mrs Sharp was quite as kind to him as she was to Gwendolen. Town Councillors and their wives called several times a week and patted him on the head in the parlour. They sent him and Gwendolen to the best school in Wolvercote. Cat was happy there. The only drawback was that Cat was left-handed, and schoolmasters always punished him if they caught him writing with his left hand. But they did that at all the schools Cat had been to, and he was used to it. He had dozens of friends. All the same, at the heart of everything, he felt lost and lonely. So he clung to Gwendolen, because she was the only family he had.

Gwendolen was often rather impatient with him, though usually she was too busy and happy to be downright cross. 'Just leave me alone, Cat,' she would say. 'Or else.' Then she would pack exercise books into a music-case and hasten next door for a lesson with Mr Nostrum.

Mr Nostrum was delighted to teach

Gwendolen for the letters. Mrs Sharp gave him one every term for a year, starting with the last. 'Not all at once, in case he gets greedy,' she said. 'And we'll give him the best last.'

Gwendolen made excellent progress. Such a promising witch was she, indeed, that she skipped the First Grade Magic exam and went straight on to the Second. She took the Third and Fourth Grades together just after Christmas, and, by the following summer, she was starting on Advanced Magic. Mr Nostrum regarded her as his favourite pupil—he told Mrs Sharp so over the wall—and Gwendolen always came back from her lessons with him pleased and golden and glowing. She went to Mr Nostrum two evenings a week, with her magic-case under her arm, just as many people might go to music-lessons. In fact, music-lessons were what Mrs Sharp put Gwendolen down as having, on the accounts she kept for the Town Council. Since Mr Nostrum never got paid, except by the letters, Cat thought this was rather dishonest of Mrs Sharp.

'I have to put something by for my old

age,' Mrs Sharp told him crossly. 'I don't get much for myself out of keeping you, do I? And I can't trust your sister to remember me when she's grown up and famous. Oh dear me no—I've no illusions about that!'

Cat knew Mrs Sharp was probably right. He was a little sorry for her, for she had certainly been kind, and he knew by now that she was not a very good witch herself. The *Certified Witch* which the notice in Mrs Sharp's parlour window claimed her to be was, in fact, the very lowest qualification. People only came to Mrs Sharp for charms when they could not afford the three Accredited Witches further down the street. Mrs Sharp eked out her earnings by acting as an agent for Mr Larkins at the junk-shop. She got him Exotic Supplies—that is to say, the stranger ingredients needed for spells—from as far away as London. She was very proud of her contacts in London. 'Oh yes,' she often said to Gwendolen, 'I've got the contacts, I have. I know those that can get me a pound of dragon's blood any time I ask, for all it's illegal. While you have me, you'll never be in need.'

Perhaps, in spite of having no illusions about Gwendolen, Mrs Sharp was really hoping to become Gwendolen's manager when Gwendolen grew up. Cat suspected she was, anyway. And he was sorry for Mrs Sharp. He was sure that Gwendolen would cast her off like an old coat when she became famous—like Mrs Sharp, Cat had no doubt that Gwendolen would be famous. So he said, 'There's me to look after you, though.' He did not fancy the idea, but he felt he ought to say it.

Mrs Sharp was warmly grateful. As a reward, she arranged for Cat to have real music-lessons. 'Then that Mayor will have nothing to complain of,' she said. She believed in killing two birds with one stone.

Cat started to learn the violin. He thought he was making good progress. He practised diligently. He never could understand why the new people living upstairs always banged on the floor when he started to play. Mrs Sharp, being tone-deaf herself, nodded and smiled while he played, and encouraged him greatly.

He was practising away one evening, when Gwendolen stormed in and shrieked a spell in his face. Cat found, to his dismay, that he was holding a large striped cat by the tail. He had its head tucked under his chin, and he was sawing at its back with the violin bow. He dropped it hurriedly. Even so, it bit him under the chin and scratched him painfully.

'What did you do that for?' he said. The cat stood in an arch, glaring at him.

'Because that's just what it sounded like!' said Gwendolen. 'I couldn't stand it a moment longer. Here, pussy, pussy!' The cat did not like Gwendolen either. It scratched the hand she held out to it. Gwendolen smacked it. It ran away, with Cat in hot pursuit, shouting, 'Stop it! That's my fiddle! Stop it!' But the cat escaped, and that was the end of the violin lessons.

Mrs Sharp was very impressed with this display of talent from Gwendolen. She climbed on a chair in the yard and told Mr Nostrum about it over the wall.

From there, the story spread to every witch and necromancer in the neighbourhood.

That neighbourhood was full of witches. People in the same trade like to cluster together. If Cat came out of Mrs Sharp's front door and turned right down Coven Street, he passed, besides the three *Accredited Witches*, two *Necromancy Offered*, a *Soothsayer*, a *Diviner*, and a *Willing Warlock*. If he turned left, he passed MR HENRY NOSTRUM A.R.C.M. *Tuition in Necromancy*, a *Fortune-Teller*, a *Sorcery For All Occasions*, a *Clairvoyant*, and lastly Mr Larkins' shop. The air in the street, and for several streets around, was heavy with the scent of magic being done.

All these people took a great and friendly interest in Gwendolen. The story of the cat impressed them enormously. They made a great pet of the creature—naturally, it was called Fiddle. Though it remained bad-tempered, captious and unfriendly, it never went short of food. They made an even greater pet of Gwendolen. Mr

Larkins gave her presents. The Willing Warlock, who was a muscular young man always in need of a shave, popped out of his house whenever he saw Gwendolen passing and presented her with a bullseye. The various witches were always looking out simple spells for her.

Gwendolen was very scornful of these spells. 'Do they think I'm a baby or something? I'm *miles* beyond this stuff!' she would say, casting the latest spell aside.

Mrs Sharp, who was glad of any aid to witchcraft, usually gathered the spell up carefully and hid it. But once or twice, Cat found the odd spell lying about. Then he could not resist trying it. He would have liked to have had just a little of Gwendolen's talent. He always hoped that he was a late-developer and that, some day, a spell would work for him. But they never did—not even the one for turning brass buttons to gold, which Cat particularly fancied.

The various fortune-tellers gave Gwendolen presents too. She got an old crystal ball from the Diviner and a pack of cards from the Soothsayer. The Fortune-Teller told her fortune for her. Gwendolen came in golden and exultant from that.

'I'm going to be famous! He said I could rule the world if I go the right way about it!' she told Cat.

Though Cat had no doubt that Gwendolen would be famous, he could not see how she could rule the world, and he said so. 'You'd only rule one country, even if you married the King,' he objected. 'And the Prince of Wales got married last year.'

'There are more ways of ruling than that, stupid!' Gwendolen retorted. 'Mr Nostrum has lots of ideas for me, for a start. Mind you, there are some snags. There's a change for the worse that I have to surmount, and a dominant Dark Stranger. But when he told me I'd rule the world my fingers all twitched, so I *know* it's true!' There seemed no limit to Gwendolen's glowing confidence.

The next day, Miss Larkins the Clairvoyant called Cat into her house and offered to tell his fortune too.

CHAPTER TWO

Cat was alarmed by Miss Larkins. She was the daughter of Mr Larkins at the junk-shop. She was young and pretty and fiercely red-headed. She wore the red hair piled into a bun on top of her head, from which red tendrils of hair escaped and tangled becomingly with earrings like hoops for parrots to sit on. She was a very talented clairvoyant, and, until the story of the cat became known. Miss Larkins had been the pet of the neighbourhood. Cat remembered that even his mother had given Miss Larkins presents.

Cat knew Miss Larkins was offering to tell his fortune out of jealousy of Gwendolen. 'No. No, thank you very much,' he said, backing away from Miss Larkins' little table spread with objects of divination. 'It's quite all right. I don't want to know.'

But Miss Larkins advanced on him and seized him by his shoulders. Cat squirmed. Miss Larkins used a scent that shrieked *VIOLETS!* at him, her earrings swung like manacles, and her corsets creaked when she was close to. 'Silly boy!' Miss Larkins said, in her rich, melodious voice. 'I'm not going to hurt you. I just want to *know*.'

'But—but I don't,' Cat said, twisting this way and that.

'Hold still,' said Miss Larkins, and tried to stare deep into Cat's eyes.

Cat shut his eyes hastily. He squirmed harder than ever. He might have got loose, had not Miss Larkins abruptly gone off into some kind of trance. Cat found himself being gripped with a strength that would have surprised him even in the Willing Warlock. He opened his eyes to find Miss Larkins staring blankly at him. Her body shook, creaking her corsets like old doors swinging in the wind. 'Oh, please let go!' Cat said. But Miss Larkins did not appear to hear. Cat took hold of the fingers gripping his shoulder and tried to prise them loose. He could not move them. After that, he could only stare helplessly at Miss Larkins' blank face.

Miss Larkins opened her mouth, and

quite a different voice came out. It was a man's voice, brisk and kindly. 'You've taken a weight off my mind, lad,' it said. It sounded pleased. 'There'll be a big change coming up for you now. But you've been awfully careless—four gone already, and only five left. You must take more care. You're in danger from at least two directions, did you know?'

The voice stopped. By this time, Cat was so frightened that he dared not move. He could only wait until Miss Larkins came to herself, yawned, and let go of him in order to cover her mouth elegantly with one hand.

'There,' she said, in her usual voice. 'That was it. What did I say?'

Finding Miss Larkins had no idea what she had said brought Cat out in goose pimples. All he wanted to do was to run away. He dashed for the door.

Miss Larkins pursued him, seized his arms again and shook him. 'Tell me! Tell me! What did I say?' With the violence of her shaking, her red hair came down in sheets. Her corsets sounded like bending planks. She was terrifying. 'What voice did I use?' she

23

demanded.

'A—a man's voice,' Cat faltered. 'Sort of nice, and no nonsense about it.'

Miss Larkins seemed dumbfounded. 'A *man*? Not Bobby or Doddo—not a child's voice, I mean?'

'No,' said Cat.

'How peculiar!' said Miss Larkins. 'I never use a man. What did he say?'

Cat repeated what the voice had said. He thought he would never forget it if he lived to ninety.

It was some consolation to find that Miss Larkins was quite as puzzled by it as he was. 'Well, I suppose it was a warning,' she said dubiously. She also seemed disappointed. 'And nothing else? Nothing about your sister?'

'No, nothing,' said Cat.

'Oh well, can't be helped,' Miss Larkins said discontentedly, and she let go of Cat in order to put her hair up again.

As soon as both her hands were safely occupied in pinning her bun, Cat ran. He shot out into the street, feeling very shaken.

And he was caught by two more

24

people almost at once.

'Ah. Here is young Eric Chant now,' said Mr Nostrum, advancing down the pavement. 'You are acquainted with my brother William, are you, young Cat?'

Cat was once more caught by an arm. He tried to smile. It was not that he disliked Mr Nostrum. It was just that Mr Nostrum always talked in this jocular way and called him 'Young Chant' every few words, which made it very difficult to talk to Mr Nostrum in return. Mr Nostrum was small and plumpish, with two wings of grizzled hair. He had a cast in his left eye, too, which always stared out sideways. Cat found that added to the difficulty of talking to Mr Nostrum. Was he looking and listening? Or was his mind elsewhere with that wandering eye?

'Yes—yes, I've met your brother,' Cat reminded Mr Nostrum. Mr William Nostrum came to visit his brother regularly. Cat saw him almost once a month. He was quite a well-to-do wizard, with a practice in Eastbourne. Mrs Sharp claimed that Mr Henry Nostrum sponged on his wealthier brother, both for money and for spells that worked. Whatever the truth of that, Cat found Mr William Nostrum even harder to talk to than his brother. He was half as large again as Mr Henry and always wore morning dress with a huge silver watch-chain across his tubby waistcoat. Otherwise, he was the image of Mr Henry Nostrum, except that both his eyes were out of true. Cat always wondered how Mr William saw anything. 'How do you do, sir,' he said to him politely.

'Very well,' said Mr William in a deep gloomy voice, as if the opposite was true.

Mr Henry Nostrum glanced up at him apologetically. 'The fact is, young Chant,' he explained, 'we have met with a little setback. My brother is upset.' He lowered his voice, and his wandering eye wandered all round Cat's right side. 'It's about those letters from—You Know Who. We can find out nothing. It seems Gwendolen knows nothing. Do you, young Chant, perchance know why your esteemed and lamented father should be acquainted with—with, let us call him, the August Personage who signed them?'

'I haven't the faintest idea, I'm afraid,' said Cat.

'Could he have been some relation?' suggested Mr Henry Nostrum. 'Chant is a Good Name.'

'I think it must be a bad name, too,' Cat answered. 'We haven't any relations.'

'But what of your dear mother?' persisted Mr Nostrum, his odd eye travelling away, while his brother managed to stare gloomily at the pavement and the rooftops at once.

'You can see the poor boy knows nothing, Henry,' Mr William said. 'I doubt if he would be able to tell us his dear mother's maiden name.'

'Oh, I do know that,' said Cat. 'It's on their marriage lines. She was called Chant too.'

'Odd,' said Mr Nostrum, swirling an eye at his brother.

'Odd, and peculiarly unhelpful,' Mr William agreed.

Cat wanted to get away. He felt he had taken enough strange questions to last till Christmas. 'Well, if you want to know that badly,' he said, 'why don't you write and ask Mr—er—Mr Chres—'

'*Hush!*' said Mr Henry Nostrum violently.

'Hum!' said his brother, almost equally violently.

'August Personage, I mean,' Cat said, looking at Mr William in alarm. Mr William's eyes had gone right to the sides of his face. Cat was afraid he might be going off into a trance, like Miss Larkins.

'It will serve, Henry, it will serve!' Mr William cried out. And, with great triumph, he lifted the silver watch-chain off his middle and shook it. 'Then for silver!' he cried.

'I'm so glad,' Cat said politely. 'I have to be going now.' He ran off down the street as fast as he could. When he went out that afternoon, he took care to turn right and go out of Coven Street past the Willing Warlock's house. It was rather a nuisance, since that was the long way round to where most of his friends lived, but anything was better than meeting Miss Larkins or the Nostrums again. It was almost enough to make Cat wish that school had started.

★   ★   ★

When Cat came home that evening, Gwendolen was just back from her lesson with Mr Nostrum. She had her usual glowing, exulting look, but she was looking secretive and important too.

'That was a good idea of yours of writing to Chrestomanci,' she said to Cat. 'I can't think why I didn't think of it. Anyway, I just have.'

'Why did you do it? Couldn't Mr Nostrum?' Cat asked.

'It came more naturally from me,' said Gwendolen. 'And I suppose it doesn't matter if he gets my signature. Mr Nostrum told me what to write.'

'Why does he want to know anyway?' Cat said.

'Wouldn't you like to know!' Gwendolen said exultingly.

'No,' said Cat. 'I wouldn't.' Since this had brought what happened that morning into his mind, which still made him almost wish the Autumn term had started, he said, 'I wish the conkers

29

were ripe.'

'Conkers!' Gwendolen said, in the greatest disgust. 'What a low mind you have! They won't be ready for a good six weeks.'

'I know,' said Cat, and for the next two days he carefully turned right every time he left the house.

They were the lovely golden days that happen when August is passing into September. Cat and his friends went out along the river. On the second day, they found a wall and climbed it. There was an orchard beyond, and here they were lucky enough to discover a tree loaded with sweet white apples—the kind that ripen early. They filled their pockets and then their hats. Then a furious gardener chased them with a rake. They ran. Cat was very happy as he carried his full, knobby hat home. Mrs Sharp loved apples. He just hoped she would not reward him by making gingerbread men. As a rule, gingerbread men were fun. They leapt up off the plate and ran when you tried to eat them, so that when you finally caught them you felt quite justified in eating them. It was a fair fight, and some got away. But Mrs Sharp's gingerbread men never did that. They simply lay, feebly waving their arms, and Cat never had the heart to eat them.

Cat was so busy thinking of all this that, though he noticed a four-wheel cab standing in the road as he turned the corner by the Willing Warlock's house, he paid no attention to it. He went to the side-door and burst into the kitchen with his hatful of apples, shouting, 'I say! Look what I've got, Mrs Sharp!'

Mrs Sharp was not there. Instead, standing in the middle of the kitchen, was a tall and quite extraordinarily well-dressed man.

Cat stared at him in some dismay. He was clearly a rich new Town Councillor. Nobody but those kind of people wore trousers with such pearly stripes, or coats of such beautiful velvet, or carried tall hats as shiny as their boots. The man's hair was dark. It was smooth as his hat. Cat had no doubt that this was Gwendolen's Dark Stranger, come to help her start ruling the world. And he should not have been in the kitchen at

31

all. Visitors were always taken straight to the parlour.

'Oh, how do you do, sir. Will you come this way, sir?' he gasped.

The Dark Stranger gave him a wondering look. And well he might, Cat thought, looking round distractedly. The kitchen was in its usual mess. The range was all ash. On the table, Cat saw, to his further dismay, Mrs Sharp had been making gingerbread men. The ingredients for the spell lay on one end of the table—all grubby newspaper packets and seedy little jars—and the gingerbread itself was strewn over the middle of the table. At the far end, the flies were gathering round the meat for lunch, which looked nearly as messy as the spell.

'Who are you?' said the Dark Stranger. 'I have a feeling I should know you. What have you got in your hat?'

Cat was too busy staring round to attend properly, but he caught the last question. His pleasure returned. 'Apples,' he said, showing the Stranger. 'Lovely sweet ones. I've been scrumping.'

The Stranger looked grave. 'Scrumping,' he said, 'is a form of stealing.'

Cat knew that as well as he did. He thought it was very joyless, even for a Town Councillor, to point it out. 'I know. But I bet you did it when you were my age.'

The Stranger coughed slightly and changed the subject. 'You haven't said yet who you are.'

'Sorry. Didn't I?' said Cat. 'I'm Eric Chant—only they always call me Cat.'

'Then is Gwendolen Chant your sister?' the Stranger asked. He was looking more and more austere and pitying. Cat suspected that he thought Mrs Sharp's kitchen was a den of vice.

'That's right. Won't you come this way?' Cat said, hoping to get the Stranger out of it. 'It's neater through here.'

'I had a letter from your sister,' the Stranger said, standing where he was. 'She gave me the impression you had drowned with your parents.'

'You must have made a mistake,' Cat said distractedly. 'I didn't drown because I was holding on to Gwendolen, and she's a witch. It's cleaner through here.'

'I see,' said the Stranger. 'I'm called Chrestomanci, by the way.'

'Oh!' said Cat. This was a real crisis. He put his hat of apples down in the middle of the spell, which he very much hoped would ruin it. 'Then you've got to come in the parlour at once.'

'Why?' said Chrestomanci, sounding rather bewildered.

'Because,' said Cat, thoroughly exasperated, 'you're far too important to stay here.'

'What makes you think I'm important?' Chrestomanci asked, still bewildered.

Cat was beginning to want to shake him. 'You must be. You're wearing important clothes. And Mrs Sharp said you were. She said Mr Nostrum would give his eyes just for your three letters.'

'*Has* Mr Nostrum given his eyes for my letters?' asked Chrestomanci. 'It hardly seems worth it.'

'No. He just gave Gwendolen lessons for them,' said Cat.

34

'What? For his eyes? How uncomfortable!' said Chrestomanci.

Fortunately, there were thumping footsteps just then, and Gwendolen burst in through the kitchen door, panting, golden and jubilant. 'Mr Chrestomanci?'

'Just Chrestomanci,' said the Stranger. 'Yes. Would you be Gwendolen?'

'Yes. Mr Nostrum told me there was a cab here,' gasped Gwendolen.

She was followed by Mrs Sharp, nearly as breathless. The two of them took over the conversation, and Cat was thankful for it. Chrestomanci at last consented to be taken to the parlour, where Mrs Sharp deferentially offered him a cup of tea and a plate of her weakly waving gingerbread men. Chrestomanci, Cat was interested to see, did not seem to have the heart to eat them either. He drank a cup of tea—austerely, without milk or sugar—and asked questions about how Gwendolen and Cat came to be living with Mrs Sharp. Mrs Sharp tried to give the impression that she looked after them for nothing, out of the goodness of her heart. She hoped Chrestomanci might be induced to pay her for their keep, as well as the Town Council.

But Gwendolen had decided to be radiantly honest. 'The town pays,' she said, 'because everyone's so sorry about the accident.' Cat was glad she had explained, even though he suspected that Gwendolen might already be casting Mrs Sharp off like an old coat.

'Then I must go and speak to the Mayor,' Chrestomanci said, and he stood up, dusting his splendid hat on his elegant sleeve. Mrs Sharp sighed and sagged. She knew what Gwendolen was doing, too. 'Don't be anxious, Mrs Sharp,' said Chrestomanci. 'No one wishes you to be out of pocket.' Then he shook hands with Gwendolen and Cat and said, 'I should have come to see you before, of course. Forgive me. Your father was so infernally rude to me, you see. I'll see you again, I hope.' Then he went away in his cab, leaving Mrs Sharp very sour, Gwendolen jubilant, and Cat nervous.

'Why are you so happy?' Cat asked

Gwendolen.

'Because he was touched at our orphaned state,' said Gwendolen. 'He's going to adopt us. My fortune is made!'

'Don't talk such nonsense!' snapped Mrs Sharp. 'Your fortune is the same as it ever was. He may have come here in all his finery, but he said nothing and he promised nothing.'

Gwendolen smiled confidently. 'You didn't see the heart-wringing letter I wrote.'

'Maybe. But he's not got a heart to wring,' Mrs Sharp retorted. Cat rather agreed with Mrs Sharp—particularly as he had an uneasy feeling that, before Gwendolen and Mrs Sharp arrived, he had somehow managed to offend Chrestomanci as badly as his father once did. He hoped Gwendolen would not realise. He knew she would be furious with him.

But, to his astonishment, Gwendolen proved to be right. The Mayor called that afternoon and told them that Chrestomanci had arranged for Cat and Gwendolen to come and live with him as part of his own family. 'And I see I needn't tell you what lucky little people you are,' he said, as Gwendolen uttered a shriek of joy and hugged the dour Mrs Sharp.

Cat felt more nervous than ever. He tugged the Mayor's sleeve. 'If you please, sir, I don't understand who Chrestomanci is.'

The Mayor patted him kindly on the head. 'A very eminent gentleman,' he said. 'You'll be hobnobbing with all the crowned heads of Europe before long, my boy. What do you think of that, eh?'

Cat did not know what to think. This had told him precisely nothing, and made him more nervous than ever. He supposed Gwendolen must have written a very touching letter indeed.

So the second great change came about in Cat's life, and very dismal he feared it would be. All that next week, while they were hurrying about being bought new clothes by Councillors' wives, and while Gwendolen grew more and more excited and triumphant, Cat found he was missing Mrs Sharp, and everyone else, even Miss Larkins, as if he had already left them. When the time came for them to get on the train, the town gave them a splendid send-off, with flags and a brass band. It upset Cat. He sat tensely on the edge of his seat, fearing he was in for a time of strangeness and maybe even misery.

Gwendolen, however, spread out her smart new dress and arranged her nice new hat becomingly, and sank elegantly back in her seat. 'I did it!' she said joyously. 'Cat, isn't it marvellous!'

'No,' Cat said miserably. 'I'm homesick already. What have you done? Why do you keep being so happy?'

'You wouldn't understand,' said Gwendolen. 'But I'll tell you part of it. I've got out of dead-and-alive Wolvercote at last—stupid Councillors and piffling necromancers! And Chrestomanci was bowled over by me. You saw that, didn't you?'

'I didn't notice specially,' said Cat. 'I mean, I saw you were being nice to him—'

'Oh, shut up, or I'll give you worse than cramps!' said Gwendolen. And, as the train at last chuffed and began to draw out of the station, Gwendolen waved her gloved hand to the brass band, up and down, just like Royalty. Cat realised she was setting out to rule the world.

CHAPTER THREE

The train journey lasted about an hour, before the train puffed into Bowbridge, where they were to get out.

'It's frightfully small,' Gwendolen said critically.

'Bowbridge!' shouted a porter, running along the platform. 'Bowbridge. The young Chants alight here, please.'

'Young Chants!' Gwendolen said disdainfully. 'Can't they treat me with more respect?' All the same, the attention pleased her. Cat could see that, as she drew on her ladylike gloves, she was shaking with excitement. He cowered behind her as they got out and watched their trunks being tossed out on to the windy platform. Gwendolen marched up to the shouting porter. '*We*

40

are the young Chants,' she told him magnificently.

It fell a little flat. The porter simply beckoned and scurried away to the entrance lobby, which was windier even than the platform. Gwendolen had to hold her hat on. Here, a young man strode towards them in a billow of flapping coat.

'*We* are the young Chants,' Gwendolen told him.

'Gwendolen and Eric? Pleased to meet you,' said the young man. 'I'm Michael Saunders. I'll be tutoring you with the other children.'

'*Other* children?' Gwendolen asked him haughtily. But Mr Saunders was evidently one of those people who are not good at standing still. He had already darted off to see about their trunks. Gwendolen was a trifle annoyed. But when Mr Saunders came back and led them outside into the station yard, they found a motor car waiting—long, black and sleek. Gwendolen forgot her annoyance. She felt this was entirely fitting.

Cat wished it had been a carriage. The

car jerked and thrummed and smelt of petrol. He felt sick almost at once. He felt sicker still when they left Bowbridge and thrummed along a winding country road. The only advantage he could see was that the car went very quickly. After only ten minutes, Mr Saunders said, 'Look—there's Chrestomanci Castle now. You get the best view from here.'

Cat turned his sick face and Gwendolen her fresh one the way he pointed. The Castle was grey and turreted, on the opposite hill. As the road turned, they saw it had a new part, with a spread of big windows, and a flag flying above. They could see grand trees—dark, layered cedars and big elms—and glimpse lawns and flowers.

'It looks marvellous,' Cat said sickly, rather surprised that Gwendolen had said nothing. He hoped the road did not wind too much in getting to the Castle.

It did not. The car flashed round a village green and between big gates. Then there was a long tree-lined avenue, with the great door of the old part of the Castle at the end of it. The car scrunched round on the gravel sweep in front of it.

Gwendolen leant forward eagerly, ready to be first one out. It was clear there would be a butler, and perhaps footmen too. She could hardly wait to make her grand entry.

But the car went on, past the grey, knobbly walls of the old Castle, and stopped at an obscure door where the new part began. It was almost a secretive door. There was a mass of rhododendron trees hiding it from both parts of the Castle.

'I'm taking you in this way,' Mr Saunders explained cheerfully, 'because it's the door you'll be using mostly, and I thought it would help you find your way about if you start as you mean to go on.'

Cat did not mind. He thought this door looked more homely. But Gwendolen, cheated of her grand entry, threw Mr Saunders a seething look and wondered whether to say a most unpleasant spell at him. She decided against it. She was still wanting to give a good impression. They got out of the car and followed Mr Saunders—whose coat had a way of billowing even when there was no wind—into a square polished passageway indoors. A most imposing lady was waiting there to meet them. She was wearing a tight purple dress, and her hair was in a very tall jet-black pile. Cat thought she must be Mrs Chrestomanci.

'This is Miss Bessemer, the housekeeper,' said Mr Saunders. 'Eric and Gwendolen, Miss Bessemer. Eric's a bit car-sick, I'm afraid.'

Cat had not realised his trouble was so obvious. He was embarrassed. Gwendolen, who was very annoyed to be met by a mere housekeeper, held her hand out coldly to Miss Bessemer.

Miss Bessemer shook hands like an Empress. Cat was just thinking she was the most awe-inspiring lady he had ever met, when she turned to him with a very kind smile. 'Poor Eric,' she said. 'Riding in a car bothers me ever so, too. You'll be all right now you're out of the thing—but if you're not, I'll give you something for it. Come and get washed, and have a look-see at your rooms.'

They followed the narrow purple triangle of her dress up some stairs, along corridors, and up more stairs. Cat had never seen anywhere so luxurious.

There was carpet the whole way—a soft green carpet, like grass in the dewy morning—and the floor at the sides was polished so that it reflected the carpet and the clean white walls and the pictures hung on the walls. Everywhere was very quiet. They heard nothing the whole way, except their own feet and Miss Bessemer's purple rustle.

Miss Bessemer opened a door on to a blaze of afternoon sun. 'This is your room, Gwendolen. Your bathroom opens off it.'

'Thank you,' said Gwendolen, and she sailed magnificently in to take possession of it. Cat peeped past Miss Bessemer and saw the room was very big, with a rich, soft Turkey carpet covering most of the floor.

Miss Bessemer said, 'The Family dines early when there are no visitors, so that they can eat with the children. But I expect you'd like some tea all the same. Whose room shall I have it sent to?'

'Mine, please,' Gwendolen said at once.

There was a short pause before Miss Bessemer said, 'Well, that's settled then, isn't it? Your room is up here, Eric.'

The way was up a twisting staircase. Cat was pleased. It looked as if his room was going to be part of the old Castle. And he was right. When Miss Bessemer opened the door, the room beyond was round, and the three windows showed that the wall was nearly three feet thick. Cat could not resist racing across the glowing carpet to scramble on one of the deep window-seats and look out. He found he could see across the flat tops of the cedars to a great lawn like a sheet of green velvet, with flower gardens going down the hillside in steps beyond it. Then he looked round the room itself. The curved walls were whitewashed, and so was the thick fireplace. The bed had a patchwork quilt on it. There was a table, a chest-of-drawers and a bookcase with interesting-looking books in it.

'Oh, I like this!' he said to Miss Bessemer.

'I'm afraid your bathroom is down the passage,' said Miss Bessemer, as if this was a drawback. But, as Cat had never had a private bathroom before, he did not mind in the least.

As soon as Miss Bessemer had gone, he hastened along to have a look at it. To his awe, there were three sizes of red towel and a sponge as big as a melon. The bath had feet like a lion's. One corner of the room was tiled, with red rubber curtains, for a shower. Cat could not resist experimenting. The bathroom was rather wet by the time he had finished. He went back to his room, a little damp himself. His trunk and box were there by this time, and a maid with red hair was unpacking them. She told Cat her name was Mary, and wanted to know if she was putting things in the right places. She was perfectly pleasant, but Cat was very shy of her. The red hair reminded him of Miss Larkins, and he could not think what to say to her.

'Er—may I go down and have some tea?' he stammered.

'Please yourself,' she said—rather coldly, Cat thought. He ran downstairs again, feeling he might have got off on the wrong foot with her.

Gwendolen's trunk was standing in the middle of her room. Gwendolen herself was sitting in a very queenly way

47

at a round table by the window, with a big pewter teapot in front of her, a plate of brown bread and butter, and a plate of biscuits.

'I told the girl I'd unpack for myself,' she said. 'I've got secrets in my trunk and my box. And I asked her to bring tea at once because I'm starving. And just look at it! Did you ever see anything so dull? Not even jam!'

'Perhaps the biscuits are nice,' Cat said hopefully. But they were not, or not particularly.

'We shall starve, in the midst of luxury!' sighed Gwendolen.

Her room was certainly luxurious. The wallpaper seemed to be made of blue velvet. The top and bottom of the bed was upholstered like a chair, in blue velvet with buttons in it, and the blue velvet bedspread matched it exactly. The chairs were painted gold. There was a dressing-table fit for a princess, with little golden drawers, gold-backed brushes, and a long oval mirror surrounded by a gilded wreath. Gwendolen admitted that she liked the dressing-table, though she was not so sure about the wardrobe, which had painted garlands and maypole-dancers on it.

'It's to hang clothes in, not to look at,' she said. 'It distracts me. But the bathroom is lovely.'

The bathroom was tiled with blue and white tiles, and the bath was sunk down into the tiled floor. Over it, draped like a baby's cradle, were blue curtains for when you wanted a shower. The towels matched the tiles. Cat preferred his own bathroom, but that may have been because he had to spend rather a long time in Gwendolen's. Gwendolen locked him in it while she unpacked. Through the hiss of the shower—Gwendolen had only herself to blame that she found her bathroom thoroughly soaked afterwards—Cat heard her voice raised in annoyance at someone who had come in to take the dull tea away and caught her with her trunk open. When Gwendolen finally unlocked the bathroom door, she was still angry.

'I don't think the servants here are very civil,' she said. 'If that girl says one thing more, she'll find herself with a boil on her nose—even if her name is Euphemia! Though,' Gwendolen added charitably, 'I'm inclined to think being called Euphemia is punishment enough for anyone. You have to go and get your new suit on, Cat. She says dinner's in half an hour and we have to change for it. Did you ever hear anything so formal and unnatural!'

'I thought you were looking forward to that kind of thing,' said Cat, who most certainly was not.

'You can be grand *and* natural,' Gwendolen retorted. But the thought of the coming grandeur soothed her all the same. 'I shall wear my blue dress with the lace collar,' she said. 'And I do think being called Euphemia is a heavy enough burden for anyone to bear, however rude they are.'

★   ★   ★

As Cat went up his winding stair, the Castle filled with a mysterious booming. It was the first noise he had heard. It alarmed him. He learnt later that it was the dressing-gong, to warn the Family that they had half an hour to change in. Cat, of course, did not take nearly that time to put his suit on. So he had yet another shower. He felt damp and weak and almost washed out of existence by the time the maid who was so unfortunate in being called Euphemia came to take him and Gwendolen downstairs to the drawing room where the Family was waiting.

Gwendolen, in her pretty blue dress, sailed in confidently. Cat crept behind. The room seemed full of people. Cat had no idea how all of them came to be part of the Family. There was an old lady in lace mittens, and a small man with large eyebrows and a loud voice who was talking about stocks and shares; Mr Saunders, whose wrists and ankles were too long for his shiny black suit; and at least two younger ladies; and at least two younger men. Cat saw Chrestomanci, quite splendid in very dark red velvet; and Chrestomanci saw Cat and Gwendolen and looked at them with a vague, perplexed smile, which made Cat quite sure that Chrestomanci had forgotten who they were.

'Oh,' said Chrestomanci. 'Er. This is my wife.'

They were ushered in front of a plump lady with a mild face. She had a gorgeous lace dress on—Gwendolen's eyes swept up and down it with considerable awe— but otherwise she was one of the most ordinary ladies they had ever seen. She gave them a friendly smile. 'Eric and Gwendolen, isn't it? You must call me Milly, my dears.' This was a relief, because neither of them had any idea what they should have called her. 'And now you must meet my Julia and my Roger,' she said.

Two plump children came and stood beside her. They were both rather pale and had a tendency to breathe heavily. The girl wore a lace dress like her mother's, and the boy had on a blue velvet suit, but no clothes could disguise the fact that they were even more ordinary-looking than their mother. They looked politely at Gwendolen and at Cat, and all four said, 'How do you do?' Then there seemed nothing else to say.

Luckily, they had not stood there long

before a butler came and opened the double doors at the end of the room, and told them that dinner was served. Gwendolen looked at this butler in great indignation. 'Why didn't he open the door to *us*?' she whispered to Cat, as they all went in a ragged sort of procession to the dining room. 'Why were we fobbed off with the housekeeper?'

Cat did not answer. He was too busy clinging to Gwendolen. They were being arranged round a long polished table, and if anyone had tried to put Cat in a chair that was not next to Gwendolen's he thought he would have fainted from terror. Luckily, no one tried. Even so, the meal was terrifying enough. Footmen kept pushing delicious food in silver plates over Cat's left shoulder. Each time that happened, it took Cat by surprise, and he jumped and jogged the plate. He was supposed to help himself off the silver plate, and he never knew how much he was allowed to take. But the worst difficulty was that he was left-handed. The spoon and fork that he was supposed to lift the food with from the footman's plate to his own were always the wrong way round. He tried changing them over, and dropped a spoon. He tried leaving them as they were, and spilt gravy. The footman always said, 'Not to worry, sir,' and made him feel worse than ever.

The conversation was even more terrifying. At one end of the table, the small loud man talked endlessly of stocks and shares. At Cat's end, they talked about Art. Mr Saunders seemed to have spent the summer travelling abroad. He had seen statues and paintings all over Europe and much admired them. He was so eager that he slapped the table as he talked. He spoke of Studios and Schools, *Quattrocento* and Dutch Interiors, until Cat's head went round. Cat looked at Mr Saunders's thin, square-cheeked face and marvelled at all the knowledge behind it. Then Milly and Chrestomanci joined in. Milly recited a string of names Cat had never heard in his life before. Chrestomanci made comments on them, as if these names were intimate friends of his. Whatever the rest of the Family was like, Cat thought, Chrestomanci was not

54

ordinary. He had very black bright eyes, which were striking even when he was looking vague and dreamy. When he was interested—as he was about Art—the black eyes screwed up in a way that seemed to spill the brightness of them over the rest of his face. And, to Cat's dismay, the two children were equally interested. They kept up a mild chirp, as if they actually knew what their parents were talking about.

Cat felt crushingly ignorant. What with this talk, and the trouble over the suddenly-appearing silver plates, and the dull biscuits he had eaten for tea, he found he had no appetite at all. He had to leave half his ice-cream pudding. He envied Gwendolen for being able to sit so calmly and scornfully enjoying her food.

It was over at last. They were allowed to escape up to Gwendolen's luxurious room. There, Gwendolen sat on her upholstered bed with a bounce.

'What a childish trick!' she said. 'They were showing off just to make us feel small. Mr Nostrum warned me they would. It's to disguise the thinness of their souls. What an awful, dull wife!

And did you ever see anyone so plain and stupid as those two children! I know I'm going to hate it here. This Castle's crushing me already.'

'It may not be so bad once we get used to it,' Cat said, without hope.

'It'll be worse,' Gwendolen promised him. 'There's something about this Castle. It's a bad influence, and a deadness. It's squashing the life and the witchcraft out of me. I can hardly breathe.'

'You're imagining things,' said Cat, 'because you want to be back with Mrs Sharp.' And he sighed. He missed Mrs Sharp badly.

'No I'm not imagining it,' said Gwendolen. 'I should have thought it was strong enough even for you to feel. Go on, try. Can't you feel the deadness?'

Cat did not really need to try, to see what she meant. There was something strange about the Castle. He had thought it was simply that it was so quiet. But it was more than that: there was a softness to the atmosphere, a weightiness, as if everything they said or did was muffled under a great feather quilt. Normal sounds, like their two voices, seemed thin. There were no echoes to them. 'Yes, it is queer,' he agreed.

'It's more than queer—it's terrible,' said Gwendolen. 'I shall be lucky if I survive.' Then she added, to Cat's surprise, 'So I'm not sorry I came.'

'I am,' said Cat.

'Oh, you would need looking after!' said Gwendolen. 'All right. There's a pack of cards on the dressing-table. They're for divination really, but if we take the trumps out we can use them to play Snap with, if you like.'

CHAPTER FOUR

The same softness and silence were there when the red-haired Mary woke Cat the next morning and told him it was time to get up. Bright morning sunshine was flooding the curved walls of his room. Though Cat knew now that the Castle must be full of people, he could hear not a sound from any of them. Nor could he hear anything from outside the windows.

I know what it's like! Cat thought. It's like when it's snowed in the night. The idea made him feel so pleased and so warm that he went to sleep again.

'You really must get up, Eric,' Mary said, shaking him. 'I've run your bath, and your lessons start at nine. Make haste, or you won't have time for breakfast.'

Cat got up. He had so strong a feeling that it had snowed in the night that he was quite surprised to find his room warm in the sun. He looked out of the windows, and there were green lawns and flowers, and rooks circling the green trees, as if there had been some mistake. Mary had gone. Cat was glad, because he was not at all sure he liked her, and he was afraid of missing breakfast. When he was dressed, he went along to the bathroom and let the hot water out of the bath. Then he dashed down the twisting stairs to find Gwendolen.

'Where do we go for breakfast?' he asked her anxiously.

Gwendolen was never at her best in

the morning. She was sitting on her blue velvet stool in front of her garlanded mirror, crossly combing her golden hair. Combing her hair was another thing which always made her cross. 'I don't know and I don't care! Shut up!' she said.

'Now that's no way to speak,' said the maid called Euphemia, briskly following Cat into the room. She was rather a pretty girl, and she did not seem to find her name the burden it should have been. 'We're waiting to give you breakfast along here. Come on.'

Gwendolen hurled her comb down expressively, and they followed Euphemia to a room just along the corridor. It was a square, airy room, with a row of big windows, but, compared with the rest of the Castle, it was rather shabby. The leather chairs were battered. The grassy carpet had stains on it. None of the cupboards would shut properly. Things like clockwork trains and tennis rackets bulged out. Julia and Roger were sitting waiting at a table by the windows, in clothes as shabby as the room.

59

Mary, who was waiting there too, said, 'And about time!' and began to work an interesting lift in a cupboard by the fireplace. There was a clank. Mary opened the lift and fetched out a large plate of bread and butter and a steaming brown jug of cocoa. She brought these over to the table, and Euphemia poured each child a mug of cocoa.

Gwendolen stared from her mug to the plate of bread. 'Is this all there is?'

'What else do you want?' asked Euphemia.

Gwendolen could not find words to express what she wanted. Porridge, bacon and eggs, grapefruit, toast and kippers all occurred to her at once, and she went on staring.

'Make up your mind,' Euphemia said at last. 'My breakfast's waiting for me too, you know.'

'Isn't there any marmalade?' said Gwendolen.

Euphemia and Mary looked at one another. 'Julia and Roger are not allowed marmalade,' Mary said.

'Nobody forbade *me* to have it,' said Gwendolen. 'Get me some marmalade at once.'

Mary went to a speaking tube by the lift, and, after much rumbling and another clank, a pot of marmalade arrived. Mary brought it and put it in front of Gwendolen.

'Thank you,' Cat said fervently. He felt as strongly about it as Gwendolen—more, in fact, because he hated cocoa.

'Oh, no trouble, I'm sure!' Mary said, in what was certainly a sarcastic way, and the two maids went out.

For a while, nobody said anything. Then Roger said to Cat, 'Pass the marmalade, please.'

'You're not supposed to have it,' said Gwendolen, whose temper had not improved.

'Nobody will know if I use one of your knives,' Roger said placidly.

Cat passed him the marmalade and his knife, too. 'Why aren't you allowed it?'

Julia and Roger looked at one another in a mild, secretive way. 'We're too fat,' Julia said, calmly taking the knife and the marmalade after Roger had done with them. Cat was not surprised, when he saw how much marmalade they had managed to pile on their bread. Marmalade stood on both slices like a sticky brown cliff.

Gwendolen looked at them with disgust, and then, rather complacently, down at her trim linen dress. The contrast was certainly striking. 'Your father is such a handsome man,' she said. 'It must be such a disappointment to him that you're both pudgy and plain, like your mother.'

The two children looked at her placidly over their cliffs of marmalade. 'Oh, I wouldn't know,' said Roger.

'Pudgy is comfortable,' said Julia. 'It must be a nuisance to look like a china doll, the way you do.'

Gwendolen's blue eyes glared. She made a small sign under the edge of the table. The bread and thick marmalade whisked itself from Julia's hands and slapped itself on Julia's face, marmalade side inwards. Julia gasped a little. 'How dare you insult me!' said Gwendolen.

Julia peeled the bread slowly off her face and then fumbled out a handkerchief. Cat supposed she was going to wipe her face. But she let the marmalade stay where it was, trundling in blobs down her plump cheeks, and simply tied a knot in the handkerchief. She pulled the knot slowly tight, looking meaningly at Gwendolen while she did so. With the final pull, the half-full jug of cocoa shot steaming into the air. It hovered for a second, and then shot sideways to hang just above Gwendolen's head. Then it began to joggle itself into tipping position.

'Stop it!' gasped Gwendolen. She put up a hand to ward the jug off. The jug dodged her and went on tipping. Gwendolen made another sign and gasped out strange words. The jug took not the slightest notice. It went on tipping, until cocoa was brimming in the very end of its spout. Gwendolen tried to lean out sideways away from it. The jug simply joggled along in the air until it was hanging over her head again.

'Shall I make it pour?' Julia asked. There was a bit of a smile under the marmalade.

'You dare!' screamed Gwendolen. 'I'll tell Chrestomanci of you! I'll—oh!' She sat up straight again, and the jug followed her faithfully. Gwendolen made another grab at it, and it dodged again.

'Careful. You'll make it spill. And what a shame about your pretty dress,' Roger said, watching complacently.

'Shut up, you!' Gwendolen shouted at him, leaning out the other way, so that she was nearly in Cat's lap. Cat looked up nervously as the jug came and hovered over him too. It seemed to be going to pour.

But, at that moment, the door opened and Chrestomanci came in, wearing a flowered silk dressing-gown. It was a red and purple dressing-gown, with gold at the neck and sleeves. It made Chrestomanci look amazingly tall, amazingly thin, and astonishingly stately. He could have been an Emperor, or a particularly severe Bishop. He was smiling as he came in, but the smile vanished when he saw the jug.

The jug tried to vanish too. It fled back to the table at the sight of him, so quickly that cocoa slopped out of it on to Gwendolen's dress—which may or may not have been an accident. Julia and

Roger both looked stricken. Julia unknotted her handkerchief as if for dear life.

'Well, I *was* coming in to say good morning,' Chrestomanci said. 'But I see that it isn't.' He looked from the jug to Julia's marmalade-glistening cheeks. 'If you two ever want to eat marmalade again,' he said, 'you'd better do as you're told. And the same goes for all four of you.'

'I wasn't doing anything wrong,' Gwendolen said, as if butter—not to speak of marmalade—would not have melted in her mouth.

'Yes, you were,' said Roger.

Chrestomanci came to the end of the table and stood looking down on them, with his hands in the pockets of his noble robe. He looked so tall like that that Cat was surprised that his head was still under the ceiling. 'There's one absolute rule in this Castle,' he said, 'which it will pay you all to remember. No witchcraft of any kind is to be practised by children, unless Michael Saunders is here to supervise you. Have you understood, Gwendolen?'

'Yes,' said Gwendolen. She gripped her lips together and clenched her hands, but she was still shaking with rage. 'I refuse to keep such a silly rule!'

Chrestomanci did not seem to hear, or to notice how angry she was. He turned to Cat. 'Have you understood too, Eric?'

'Me?' Cat said in surprise. 'Yes, of course.'

'Good,' said Chrestomanci. 'Now I *will* say good morning.'

'Good morning, Daddy,' said Julia and Roger. 'Er—good morning,' Cat said. Gwendolen pretended not to hear. Two could play at that game. Chrestomanci smiled and swept out of the room like a very long procession of one person.

'Tell-tale!' Gwendolen said to Roger, as soon as the door had shut. 'And that was a dirty trick with that jug! You were both doing it, weren't you?'

Roger smiled sleepily, not in the least disturbed. 'Witchcraft runs in our family,' he said.

'And we've both inherited it,' said Julia. 'I must go and wash.' She picked up three slices of bread to keep her going while she did so, and left the room, calling over her shoulder, 'Tell Michael I won't be long, Roger.'

'More cocoa?' Roger said politely, picking up the jug.

'Yes, please,' said Cat. It never bothered him to eat or drink things that had been bewitched, and he was thirsty. He thought that if he filled his mouth with marmalade and strained the cocoa through it, he might not taste the cocoa. Gwendolen, however, was sure Roger was trying to insult her. She flounced round in her chair and stayed haughtily looking at the wall, until Mr Saunders suddenly threw open a door Cat had not noticed before and said cheerfully:

'Right, all of you. Lesson time. Come on through and see how you stand up to some grilling.'

Cat hastily swallowed his cocoa-flavoured marmalade. Beyond the door was a schoolroom. It was a real, genuine schoolroom, although there were only four desks in it. There was a blackboard, a globe, the pitted school floor and the schoolroom smell. There was that kind of glass-fronted bookcase without which

67

no schoolroom is complete, and the battered grey-green and dark blue books without which no schoolroom bookcase is complete. On the walls were big pictures of the statues Mr Saunders had found so interesting.

Two of the desks were brown and old. Two were new and yellow with varnish. Gwendolen and Cat sat silently in the new desks. Julia hurried in, with her face shining with soap, and sat in the old desk beside Roger's, and the grilling began. Mr Saunders strode gawkily up and down in front of the blackboard, asking keen questions. His tweed jacket billowed out from his back, just as his coat had done in the wind. Perhaps that was why the sleeves of the jacket were so much too short for Mr Saunders's long arms. The long arm shot out, and a foot of bony wrist with a keen finger on the end of it pointed at Cat. 'What part did witchcraft play in the Wars of the Roses?'

'Er,' said Cat. 'Ung. I'm afraid I haven't done them yet, sir.'

'Gwendolen,' said Mr Saunders.

'Oh—a very big part,' Gwendolen

guessed airily.

'Wrong,' said Mr Saunders. 'Roger.'

From the grilling, it emerged that Roger and Julia had forgotten a great deal over the summer, but, even so, they were well ahead of Cat in most things, and far ahead of Gwendolen in everything.

'What *did* you learn at school?' Mr Saunders asked her, in some exasperation.

Gwendolen shrugged. 'I've forgotten. It wasn't interesting. I was concentrating on witchcraft, and I intend to go on doing that, please.'

'I'm afraid you can't,' said Mr Saunders.

Gwendolen stared at him, hardly able to believe she had heard him right. 'What!' she almost shrieked 'But—but I'm terribly talented! I *have* to go on with it!'

'Your talents will keep,' said Mr Saunders. 'You can take up witchcraft again when you've learnt something else. Open your arithmetic book and do me the first four exercises. Eric, I think I'll set you going on some History. Write

69

me an essay on the reign of King Canute.' He moved on to set work for Roger and Julia.

Cat and Gwendolen opened books. Gwendolen's face was red, then white. As Mr Saunders bent over Roger, her inkwell sailed up out of the socket in her desk, and emptied itself over the back of Mr Saunders's billowing tweed jacket. Cat bit his lip in order not to laugh. Julia watched with calm interest. Mr Saunders did not seem to notice. The inkwell returned quietly to its socket.

'Gwendolen,' said Mr Saunders, without turning round. 'Get the ink-jar and funnel out of the bottom of the cupboard and refill that inkwell. And fill it properly, please.'

Gwendolen got up, jauntily and defiantly, found the big flask and funnel, and started to fill her inkwell. Ten minutes later, she was still pouring away. Her face was puzzled at first, then red, then white with fury again. She tried to put the flask down, and found she could not. She tried whispering a spell.

Mr Saunders turned and looked at

her.

'You're being perfectly horrible! said Gwendolen. 'Besides, I'm allowed to do witchcraft when you're here.'

'No one is allowed to pour ink over their tutor,' Mr Saunders said cheerfully. 'And I'd already told you that you've given up witchcraft for the time being. Keep on pouring till I tell you to stop.'

Gwendolen poured ink for the next half hour, and got angrier every minute of it.

Cat was impressed. He suspected that Mr Saunders was rather a powerful magician. Certainly, when he next looked at Mr Saunders, there was no sign of any ink on his back. Cat looked at Mr Saunders fairly often, to see whether it was safe to change his pen from his right to his left hand. He had been punished so often for writing left-handed that he was good at keeping an eye on his teachers. When Mr Saunders turned his way, Cat used his right hand. It was slow and reluctant. But as soon as Mr Saunders turned away again, Cat changed his pen over and got on like a house on fire. The main trouble was that, in order not to smudge the ink with his left hand, he had to hold the paper sideways. But he was pretty deft at flicking his book straight again whenever Mr Saunders seemed likely to look at him.

When the half hour was over, Mr Saunders, without turning round, told Gwendolen to stop pouring ink and do sums. Then, still without turning round, he said to Cat, 'Eric, what are you doing?'

'An essay on King Canute,' Cat said innocently.

Then Mr Saunders did turn round, but, by that time, the paper was straight and the pen in Cat's right hand. 'Which hand were you writing with?' he said. Cat was used to this. He held up his right hand with the pen in it. 'It looked like both hands to me,' Mr Saunders said, and he came over and looked at the page Cat had written. 'It *was* both.'

'It doesn't show,' Cat said miserably.

'Not much,' Mr Saunders agreed. 'Does it amuse you to write with alternate hands, or something?'

'No,' Cat confessed. 'But I'm left-handed.'

Then, as Cat had feared, Mr Saunders flew into a towering rage. His face went red. He slammed his big knobbly hand down on Cat's desk, so that Cat jumped and the inkwell jumped too, sending ink splashing over Mr Saunders's great hand and over Cat's essay. '*Left-handed*!' he roared. 'Then why the Black Gentleman don't you *write* with your left hand, boy?'

'They—they punish me if I do,' Cat faltered, very shaken, and very perplexed to find Mr Saunders was angry for such a peculiar reason.

'Then they deserve to be tied up in knots and roasted!' roared Mr Saunders, 'whoever *they* are! You're doing yourself untold harm by obeying them, boy! If I catch you writing with your right hand again, you'll be in really serious trouble!'

'Yes,' Cat said, relieved but still very shaken. He looked mournfully at his ink-splashed essay and hoped Mr Saunders might use a little witchcraft on that, too. But Mr Saunders took the book and tore the page right out.

'Now do it again properly!' he said, slapping the book back in front of Cat.

Cat was still writing all over again about Canute when Mary came in with a tray of milk and biscuits and a cup of coffee for Mr Saunders. And after the milk and biscuits, Mr Saunders told Cat and Gwendolen they were free till lunch. 'Though not because of a good morning's work,' he said. 'Go out and get some fresh air.' As they went out of the schoolroom, he turned to Roger and Julia. 'Now we'll have a little witchcraft,' he said. 'And let's hope you haven't forgotten all that, too.'

Gwendolen stopped in the doorway and looked at him.

'No. Not you,' Mr Saunders said to her. 'I told you.'

Gwendolen whirled round and ran away, through the shabby playroom and down the corridor beyond. Cat ran after her as hard as he could, but he did not catch her up until they came to a much grander part of the Castle, where a big marble staircase curled away downwards and the light came from an elegant dome in the roof.

'This isn't the right way,' Cat panted.

'Yes it is,' Gwendolen said fiercely. 'I'm going to find Chrestomanci. Why should those two fat little fools learn witchcraft and not me? I've got twice their gifts. It took two of them just to levitate a jug of cocoa! So I want Chrestomanci.'

By a stroke of good fortune, Chrestomanci was coming along the gallery on the other side of the staircase, behind a curly marble balustrade. He was wearing a fawn-coloured suit now, instead of the imperial dressing-gown, but he looked, if possible, even more elegant. By the look on his face, his thoughts were miles away. Gwendolen ran round the head of the marble staircase and stood herself in front of him. Chrestomanci blinked, and looked vaguely from her to Cat. 'Was one of you wanting me?'

'Yes. Me,' said Gwendolen. 'Mr Saunders won't give me witchcraft lessons, and I want you to tell him he must.'

'Oh, but I can't do that,' Chrestomanci said absentmindedly.

'Sorry and so on.'

Gwendolen stamped her foot. It made no noise to speak of, even there on the marble floor, and there was no echo. Gwendolen was forced to shout instead. '*Why not?* You must, you must, you *must!*'

Chrestomanci looked down at her, in a peering surprised way, as if he had only just seen her. 'You seem to be annoyed,' he said. 'But I'm afraid it's unavoidable. I told Michael Saunders that he was on no account to teach either of you witchcraft.'

'*You* did! Why *not?*' Gwendolen shouted.

'Because you were bound to misuse it, of course,' said Chrestomanci, as if it were quite obvious. 'But I'll reconsider it in a year or so, if you still want to learn.' Then he smiled kindly at Gwendolen, obviously expecting her to be pleased, and drifted dreamily away down the marble stairs.

Gwendolen kicked the marble balustrade and hurt her foot. That sent her into a rage as strong as Mr Saunders's. She danced and jumped and shrieked at the head of the stairs, until Cat was quite frightened of her. She shook her fist at Chrestomanci. 'I'll show you! You wait!' she screamed. But Chrestomanci had gone out of sight round the bend in the staircase and perhaps he could not hear. Even Gwendolen's loudest scream sounded thin and small.

Cat was puzzled. What *was* it about this Castle? He looked up at the dome where the light came in and thought that Gwendolen's screaming ought to have echoed round it like the dickens. Instead, it made a small, high squawking. While he waited for her to get her temper back, Cat experimentally put his fingers to his mouth and whistled as hard as he could. It made a queer blunt noise, like a squeaky boot. It also brought the old lady with the mittens out of a door in the gallery.

'You noisy little children!' she said. 'If you want to scream and whistle, you must go out in the grounds and do it there.'

'Oh, come on!' Gwendolen said crossly to Cat, and the two of them ran away to the part of the Castle they were used to. After a bit of muddling around, they discovered the door they had first come in by and let themselves outside through it.

'Let's explore everywhere,' said Cat. Gwendolen shrugged and said it suited her, so they set off.

Beyond the shrubbery of rhododendrons, they found themselves out on the great smooth lawn with the cedar trees. It spread across the entire front of the newer part of the Castle. On the other side of it, Cat saw the most interesting high sun-soaked old wall, with trees hanging over it. It was clearly the ruins of an even older castle. Cat set off towards it at a trot, past the big windows of the newer Castle, dragging Gwendolen with him. But, halfway there, Gwendolen stopped and stood poking at the shaved green grass with her toe.

'Hm,' she said. 'Do you think this counts as in the Castle?'

'I expect so,' said Cat. 'Do come on. I want to explore those ruins there.'

However, the first wall they came to

was a low one, and the door in it led them into a very formal garden. It had broad gravel paths, running very straight, between box hedges. There were yew trees everywhere, clipped into severe pyramids, and all the flowers were yellow, in tidy clumps.

'Boring,' said Cat, and led the way to the ruin wall beyond.

But once again there was a lower wall in the way, and this time they came out into an orchard. It was a very tidy orchard, in which all the trees were trained flat, to stand like hedges on either side of the winding gravel paths. They were loaded with apples, some of them quite big. After what Chrestomanci had said about scrumping, Cat did not quite dare pick one, but Gwendolen picked a big red Worcester and bit into it.

Instantly, a gardener appeared from round a corner and told them reproachfully that picking apples was forbidden.

Gwendolen threw the apple down in the path. 'Take it then. There was a maggot in it anyway.'

They went on, leaving the gardener staring ruefully at the bitten apple. And instead of reaching the ruins, they came to a goldfish pond, and after that to a rose garden. Here Gwendolen, as an experiment, tried picking a rose. Instantly, another gardener appeared and explained respectfully that they were not allowed to pick roses. So Gwendolen threw the rose down too. Then Cat looked over his shoulder, and discovered that the ruins were somehow behind them now. He turned back. But he still did not seem to reach them. It was nearly lunch time before he suddenly turned into a steep little path between two walls and found the ruins above him, at the top of the path.

Cat pelted joyfully up the steep path. The sun-soaked wall ahead was taller than most houses, and there were trees at the top of it. When he was close enough, Cat saw that there was a giddy stone staircase jutting out of the wall, more like a stone ladder than a stair. It was so old that snapdragons and wallflowers had rooted in it, and hollyhocks had grown up against the place where the stair met the ground. Cat had to push aside a tall red hollyhock in order to put his foot on the first stair.

No sooner had he done so than yet another gardener came puffing up the steep path. 'You can't go there! That's Chrestomanci's garden up there, that is!'

'Why can't we?' said Cat, deeply disappointed.

'Because it's not allowed, that's why.'

Slowly and reluctantly, Cat came away. The gardener stood at the foot of the stair to make sure he went. 'Bother!' Cat said.

'I'm getting rather sick of Chrestomanci forbidding things,' said Gwendolen. 'It's time someone taught him a lesson.'

'What are you going to do?' said Cat.

'Wait and see,' said Gwendolen, pressing her lips together in her stormiest way.

CHAPTER FIVE

Gwendolen refused to tell Cat what she was going to do. This meant that Cat had rather a melancholy time. After a wholesome lunch of swede and boiled mutton, they had lessons again. After that, Gwendolen ran hastily away and would not let Cat come with her. Cat did not know what to do.

'Would you care to come out and play?' Roger asked.

Cat looked at him and saw that he was just being polite. 'No thank you,' he said politely. He was forced to wander round the gardens on his own. There was a wood lower down, full of horse chestnuts, but the conkers were not nearly ripe. As Cat was half-heartedly staring up into one, he saw there was a tree-house in it, about halfway up. This was more like it. Cat was just about to climb up to it, when he heard voices and saw Julia's skirt flutter among the leaves. So that was no good. It was Julia and Roger's private tree-house, and they were in it.

Cat wandered away again. He came to the lawn, and there was Gwendolen, crouching under one of the cedars, very busy digging a small hole.

'What are you doing?' said Cat.

'Go away,' said Gwendolen.

Cat went away. He was sure what Gwendolen was doing was witchcraft and had to do with teaching Chrestomanci a lesson, but it was no good asking Gwendolen when she was being this secretive. Cat had to wait. He waited through another terrifying dinner, and then through a long, long evening. Gwendolen locked herself in her room after dinner and told him to go away when he knocked.

⋆　　⋆　　⋆

Next morning, Cat woke up early and hurried to the nearest of his three windows. He saw at once what Gwendolen had been doing. The lawn was ruined. It was not a smooth stretch of green velvet any longer. It was a mass of molehills. As far as Cat could see in both directions, there were little green mounds, little heaps of raw earth, long lines of raw earth and long green furrows of raised grass. There must have been an army of moles at work on it all night. About a dozen gardeners were standing in a gloomy huddle, scratching their heads over it.

Cat threw on his clothes and dashed downstairs.

Gwendolen was leaning out of her window in her frilly cotton nightdress, glowing with pride. 'Look at that!' she said to Cat. 'Isn't it marvellous! There's acres of it, too. It took me hours yesterday evening to make sure it was all spoilt. That will make Chrestomanci think a bit!'

Cat was sure it would. He did not know how much a huge stretch of turf like that would cost to replace, but he suspected it was a great deal. He was afraid Gwendolen would be in really bad trouble.

But, to his astonishment, nobody so much as mentioned the lawn. Euphemia came in a minute later, but all she said was, 'You'll both be late for your breakfast again.' Roger and Julia said nothing at all. They silently accepted the marmalade and Cat's knife when he passed them over, but the sole thing either of them said was when Julia dropped Cat's knife and picked it up again all fluffy. She said, 'Bother!' And when Mr Saunders called them through for lessons, the only things he talked about were what he was teaching them. Cat decided that nobody knew Gwendolen had caused the moles. They could have no idea what a strong witch she was.

There were no lessons after lunch that day. Mr Saunders explained that they always had Wednesday afternoons off. And at lunchtime, every molehill had gone. When they looked out of the playroom window, the lawn was like a sheet of velvet again.

'I don't believe it!' Gwendolen whispered to Cat. 'It must be an illusion. They're trying to make me feel small.'

They went out and looked after lunch. They had to be fairly cautious about it, because Mr Saunders was taking his afternoon off in a deckchair under one of

the cedars, reading a yellow paper-
backed book which seemed to amuse
him a great deal. Gwendolen sauntered
out into the middle of the lawn and
pretended to be admiring the Castle. She
pretended to tie her bootlace and
prodded the turf with her fingers.

'I don't understand it!' she said. Being
a witch, she knew the close, smooth turf
was no illusion. 'It really is all right!
How was it done?'

'They must have carted in new turf
while we were having lessons,' Cat
suggested.

'Don't be stupid!' said Gwendolen.
'New turf would all be in squares still,
and this isn't.'

Mr Saunders called to them.

Gwendolen looked, for a second,
more apprehensive than Cat had ever
seen her. But she hid it fairly well and
led the way casually over to the
deckchair. Cat saw that the yellow book
was in French. Fancy being able to
laugh at something in French! Mr
Saunders must be a learned magician as
well as a strong one.

Mr Saunders laid the book face down

on the once-more-beautiful grass and smiled up at them. 'You two went away so quickly that you never gave me time to dish you out your pocket-money. Here you are.' It was a crown piece—five whole shillings. He had never had so much money to spend in his life. Mr Saunders added to his amazement by saying, 'You'll get that every Wednesday. I don't know whether you're savers or spenders. What Julia and Roger usually do is to go down to the village and blue it all on sweets.'

'Thank you,' said Cat, 'very much. Shall we go down to the village, Gwendolen?'

'We may as well,' Gwendolen agreed. She was divided between a defiant desire to stay at the Castle and face whatever trouble was coming over the moles, and relief at an excuse to get away. 'I expect Chrestomanci will send for me as soon as he realises it was me,' she said as they walked down the avenue of trees.

'Do you think it was Mr Saunders who put the lawn right?' Cat asked.

Gwendolen frowned. 'He couldn't have. He was teaching us.'

'Those gardeners,' suggested Cat. 'Some of them could be warlocks. They did turn up awfully quickly to forbid us things.'

Gwendolen laughed scornfully. 'Think of the Willing Warlock.'

Cat did, a little dubiously. The Willing Warlock was not much more gifted than Mrs Sharp. He was usually hired for heavy carrying jobs, or to make the wrong horse win at the races. 'All the same,' he argued, 'they could be specialists—garden warlocks.'

Gwendolen only laughed again.

*   *   *

The village was just beyond the Castle gates, at the foot of the hills where the Castle stood. It was a pretty place, round a big green. Across the green, there were shops: a beautiful bow-fronted baker's and an equally beautiful sweetshop and Post Office. Cat wanted to visit both, but Gwendolen stopped at a third shop, which was a junk-shop. Cat did not mind going into that, either. It looked interesting. But Gwendolen shook her

88

head irritably and stopped a village boy who was loitering near it.

'I was told a Mr Baslam lives in this village. Can you tell me where he lives?'

The boy made a face. 'Him? He's no good. Down there, at the end of that alley, if you really want to know.' And he stood looking at them, with the air of someone who has earned sixpence for his pains.

Neither Cat nor Gwendolen had any money beside their crown pieces. They had to go away without giving him anything. The boy shouted after them.

'Stuck up little witch! Mingy little warlock!'

Gwendolen did not mind this in the least, but Cat was so ashamed that he wanted to go back and explain.

Mr Baslam lived in a shabby cottage with an ill-written notice propped in one window: *Eggsotick Serplys*. Gwendolen looked at it rather pityingly as she hammered on the door with the dingy knocker. When Mr Baslam opened his door, he proved to be a fat person in old trousers which sagged to make room for his fatness, and with red drooping eyes like a St Bernard's. He started to shut the door again as soon as he saw them.

'Not today, thank you,' he said, and a strong smell of beer came out with the words.

'Mr Nostrum sent me,' said Gwendolen. 'Mr William Nostrum.'

The door stopped shutting. 'Ah,' said Mr Baslam. 'Then you better both come in. This way.' He led them into a poky room containing four chairs, a table, and several dozen cases of stuffed animals. There was hardly room for all the cases of stuffed animals. They stood higgledy-piggledy, one on top of another, and they were all very dusty. 'Sit down then,' said Mr Baslam, rather grudgingly.

Cat sat down gently and tried not to breathe too deeply. Beside the beery smell from Mr Baslam, there was a faint rotting smell and a smell like pickles. Cat thought that some of the stuffed animals had not been properly cured. The smell did not seem to bother Gwendolen. She sat looking like a picture of a perfect little girl. Her cream-coloured dress spread crisply round her and her broad hat becomingly shaded her golden hair. She looked at Mr Baslam with severe blue eyes.

'I think your notice is spelt wrong.'

Mr Baslam drooped his St Bernard eyes and made gestures that were meant to be joking. 'I know. I know. But I don't want to be taken serious, do I? Not on the very threshold, as it were. Now what was you wanting? Mr William Nostrum don't tell me too much of his plans. I'm only a humble supplier.'

'I want some supplies, of course,' said Gwendolen.

Cat listened, rather bored, to Gwendolen bargaining for the materials of witchcraft. Mr Baslam fumbled in the backs of stuffed animal cases and fetched out newspaper screws of this and that—newts' eyes, snakes' tongues, cardamom, hellebore, mummy, nitre, seed of moly and various resins—which probably accounted for the unpleasant smell. He wanted more for them than Gwendolen would pay. She was determined to lay out her five shillings to the best possible advantage. Mr Baslam seemed to resent it. 'Know your own mind, don't you?' he said peevishly.

'I know how much things should cost,' said Gwendolen. She took her hat off, packed the little screws of newspaper carefully into its crown, and put it neatly back on her head again. 'And last, I think I shall be wanting some dragon's blood,' she said.

'Ooooh!' said Mr Baslam, dolefully shaking his head so that his hanging cheeks flapped. 'Dragon's blood is banned from use, young lady. You ought to know that. I don't know as I can manage you any of that.'

'Mr Nostrum—both Mr Nostrums— told me you could get *anything*,' said Gwendolen. 'They said you were the best agent they knew. And I'm not asking for dragon's blood *now*. I'm ordering some.'

Mr Baslam looked gratified at being praised by the Nostrum brothers, but he was still dubious. 'It's a fearful strong charm needs dragon's blood,' he said plaintively. 'You won't be doing anything that strong yourself, a young lady like you, now.'

'I don't know yet,' said Gwendolen.

'But I think I might. I'm on Advanced Magic, you know. And I want dragon's blood in case I need it.'

'It'll come dear,' Mr Baslam warned her. 'It's costly stuff. There's the risk to pay for, you see. I don't want the law on me.'

'I can pay,' said Gwendolen. 'I'll pay in instalments. You can take the rest of the five shillings on account.'

Mr Baslam was unable to resist this. The way he looked at the crown piece Gwendolen handed to him made Cat see vividly a long row of frothing pints of beer. 'Done,' said Mr Baslam. Gwendolen smiled graciously and got up to go. Cat thankfully leapt up too. 'What about you, young gentleman?' Mr Baslam asked wheedlingly. 'Aren't you going to try your hand at a bit of necromancy at all?'

'He's just my brother,' said Gwendolen.

'Oh. Ah. Um. Yes,' said Mr Baslam. 'He's that one, of course. Well, good day to you both. Come again, any time.'

'When will you have the dragon's blood?' Gwendolen asked him on the doorstep.

Mr Baslam thought. 'Say a week?'

Gwendolen's face glowed. 'How quick! I knew you were a good agent. Where do you get it from so quickly?'

'Now that would be telling, wouldn't it?' said Mr Baslam. 'It has to come from another world, but which one is a trade secret, young lady.'

Gwendolen was jubilant as they went back along the alley. 'A week!' she said. 'That's the quickest I've ever heard. It has to be smuggled in from this other world, you know. He must have awfully good connections there.'

'Or he's got some already, inside a stuffed bird,' said Cat, who had not liked Mr Baslam at all. 'Whatever do you want dragon's blood for? Mrs Sharp says it costs fifty pounds an ounce.'

'Be quiet,' said Gwendolen. 'Oh, quick! Hurry, Cat! Get into that sweet shop. She mustn't know where I've been.'

Out on the village green, a lady carrying a parasol was talking to a clergyman. She was Chrestomanci's wife. Cat and Gwendolen bundled themselves into the shop and hoped she had not seen them. There, Cat bought them a bag of toffee each. Milly was still there, so he bought some liquorice too. Milly was still talking to the clergyman even then, so he bought Gwendolen a penwiper and himself a postcard of the Castle. Milly was still there. But Cat could not think of anything else to buy, so they had to come out of the shop.

Milly beckoned to them as soon as they did. 'Come and meet the dear vicar.'

The vicar, who was old, with a weak and wandering look, shakily shook hands with them and said he would see them on Sunday. Then he said he really must be going now.

'And so must we,' said Milly. 'Come on, my dears. We'll walk back to the Castle together.'

There was nothing to do but walk beside her under the shadow of her parasol, across the green and between the lodge gates. Cat was afraid she was going to ask them why they had been visiting Mr Baslam. Gwendolen was sure she was going to ask her about the moles in the lawn. But what Milly said was, 'I am glad of a chance to talk to you, my loves. I haven't had a moment to see how you were getting on. Are you all right? Are you finding it very strange?'

'A—a little,' Cat admitted.

'The first few days are always the worst, anywhere,' said Milly. 'I'm sure you'll soon find your way round. And don't hesitate to use the toys in the playroom if you want. They're for everyone. Private toys are in one's own room. How are you liking your rooms?'

Cat looked up at her in astonishment. She was talking as if moles and witchcraft had never existed. Milly beamed back at him. Despite her elegant ruched dress and her lacy parasol, she was a most ordinary, kind, good-natured lady. Cat liked her. He assured Milly that he liked his room, and his bathroom—particularly the shower—and explained that he had never had a bathroom to himself before.

'Oh, I'm glad. I did so hope you'd like it,' said Milly. 'Miss Bessemer wanted to put you next to Roger, but I thought that room was so dull—and it doesn't have a

shower. Look at it some time and you'll
see what I mean.'

She walked on up the avenue,
chattering away, and Cat found himself
doing all the rest of the talking. As soon
as it was clear that Milly was not going to
mention either lawns or exotic supplies,
Gwendolen began to despise her. She
kept up a scornful silence, and left Cat to
talk. After a while, Milly asked Cat what
thing about the Castle he was finding
strangest.

Cat answered shyly, but without
hesitation, 'The way everyone talks at
supper.'

Milly let out such a yell of despair that
Cat jumped and Gwendolen was more
scornful than ever. 'Oh dear! Poor Eric!
I've seen you looking! Isn't it awful?
Michael gets these enthusiasms, and
then he can talk of nothing else. It
should be wearing off in a day or so,
though, and then we can have reasonable
talk again and make a few jokes. I like to
laugh at dinner, don't you? I'm afraid
nothing will stop poor Bernard talking
about stocks and shares, but you
mustn't take any notice of that. Nobody

listens to Bernard. Do you like eclairs, by the way?'

'Yes,' said Cat.

'Oh good!' said Milly. 'I've ordered tea for us on the lawn, since this is your first Wednesday and I didn't want to waste this lovely weather. Isn't it funny how September's nearly always fine? If we slip through the trees here, we should be on the lawn as soon as tea is.'

Sure enough, they followed Milly out of the shrubbery to find a whole cluster of deckchairs round the one where Mr Saunders was, and footmen putting out tables and carrying trays. Most of the Family were gathering among the deckchairs. Gwendolen followed Milly and Cat over, looking nervous and defiant. She knew Chrestomanci was going to speak to her about the lawn now, and, to make matters worse, she was not going to have a chance to take the exotic supplies out of her hat before he did.

But Chrestomanci was not there, though everyone else was. Milly pushed between stocks-and-shares Bernard and Julia, and past the old lady with mittens, to point her parasol sternly at Mr Saunders. 'Michael, you are absolutely forbidden to talk about Art during tea,' she said, and spoilt the sternness rather by laughing.

The Family evidently felt much the same as Cat. Several of them said 'Hear, hear!' and Roger said, 'Can we start, Mummy?'

Cat enjoyed the tea. It was the first time he had enjoyed anything since he came to the Castle. There were paper-thin cucumber sandwiches and big squashy eclairs. Cat ate even more than Roger did. He was surrounded by cheerful, ordinary chat from the Family, with a hum of stocks and shares in the background, and the sun lay warm and peaceful on the green stretches of the lawn. Cat was glad someone had somehow restored it. He liked it better smooth. He began to think he could almost be happy at the Castle, with a little practice.

Gwendolen was nothing like so happy. The newspaper packets weighed on her head. Their smell spoilt the taste of the eclairs. And she knew she would have to wait until dinner before Chrestomanci spoke to her about the lawn.

* * *

Dinner was later that night, because of the tea. Dusk was falling when they filed into the dining room. There were lighted candles all down the polished table. Cat could see them, and the rest of the room, reflected in the row of long windows facing him. It was a pleasing sight, and a useful one. Cat could see the footman coming. For once he was not taken by surprise when the man thrust a tray of little fish and pickled cabbage over his shoulder. And, as he was now forbidden to use his right hand, Cat felt quite justified in changing the serving things over. He began to feel he was settling in.

Because he had not been allowed to talk about Art at tea, Mr Saunders was more than usually eloquent at dinner. He talked and he talked. He took Chrestomanci's attention to himself, and he talked at him. Chrestomanci seemed dreamy and good-humoured. He listened and nodded. And Gwendolen grew crosser every minute. Chrestomanci said not a word about lawns, neither here nor in the drawing room beforehand. It became clearer and clearer that no one was going to mention the matter at all.

Gwendolen was furious. She wanted her powers recognised. She wanted to show Chrestomanci she was a witch to be reckoned with. So there was nothing for it but to begin on another spell. She was a little hampered by not having any ingredients to hand, but there was one thing she could do quite easily.

The dinner went on. Mr Saunders talked on. Footmen came round with the next course. Cat looked over at the windows to see when the silver plate would come to him. And he nearly screamed.

There was a skinny white creature there. It was pressed against the dark outside of the glass, mouthing and waving. It looked like the lost ghost of a lunatic. It was weak and white and loathsome. It was draggled and slimy.

Even though Cat realised almost at once that it was Gwendolen's doing, he still stared at it in horror.

Milly saw him staring. She looked herself, shuddered, and tapped Chrestomanci gently on the back of the hand with her spoon. Chrestomanci came out of his gentle dream and glanced at the window too. He gave the piteous creature a bored look, and sighed.

'And so I still think Florence is the finest of all the Italian States,' said Mr Saunders.

'People usually put in a word for Venice,' said Chrestomanci. 'Frazier, would you draw the curtains, please? Thank you.'

'No, no. In my opinion, Venice is overrated,' Mr Saunders asserted, and he went on to explain why, while the butler drew the long orange curtains and shut the creature out of sight.

'Yes, maybe you're right. Florence has more to offer,' Chrestomanci agreed. 'By the way, Gwendolen, when I said the Castle, I meant of course the Castle grounds as well as indoors. Now, do

102

carry on Michael. Venice.'

Everyone carried on, except Cat. He could imagine the creature still mouthing and fumbling at the glass behind the orange curtains. He could not eat for thinking of it.

'It's all right, stupid! I've sent it away,' said Gwendolen. Her voice was sticky with rage.

CHAPTER SIX

Gwendolen gave vent to her fury in her room after dinner. She jumped on her bed and threw cushions about, screaming. Cat stood prudently back against the wall waiting for her to finish. But Gwendolen did not finish until she had pledged herself to a campaign against Chrestomanci.

'I hate this place!' she bawled. 'They try to cover everything up in soft sweet niceness. I hate it, I hate it!' Her voice was muffled among the velvets of her room and swallowed up in the prevailing softness of the Castle. 'Do you hear it?'

Gwendolen screamed. 'It's an eiderdown of hideous niceness! I wreck their lawn, so they give me tea. I conjure up a lovely apparition, and they have the curtains drawn. *Frazier, would you draw the curtains, please!* Ugh! Chrestomanci makes me sick!'

'I didn't think it was a lovely apparition,' Cat said, shivering.

'Ha, ha! You didn't know I could do that, did you?' said Gwendolen. 'It wasn't to frighten *you*, you idiot. It was to give Chrestomanci a shock. I hate him! He wasn't even interested.'

'What did he have us to live here for, if he isn't interested in you either?' Cat wondered.

Gwendolen was rather struck by this. 'I hadn't thought of that,' she said. 'It may be serious. Go away. I want to think about it. Anyway,' she shouted, as Cat was going to the door, 'he's going to *be* interested, if it's the last thing I do! I'm going to do something every day until he notices!'

Once again, Cat was mournfully on his own. Remembering what Milly had said, he went along to the playroom. But

Roger and Julia were there, playing with soldiers on the stained carpet. The little tin grenadiers were marching about. Some were wheeling up cannon. Others were lying behind cushions, firing their rifles with little pinpricks of bangs. Roger and Julia turned round guiltily.

'You won't mention this, will you?' said Julia.

'Would you like to come and play too?' Roger asked politely.

'Oh, no thanks,' Cat sat hastily. He knew he could never join in this kind of game unless Gwendolen helped him. But he did not dare disturb Gwendolen in her present mood. And he had nothing to do. Then he remembered that Milly had obviously expected him to poke about the Castle more than he had done. So he set off to explore, feeling rather daring.

The Castle seemed strange at night. There were dim little electric lights at regular intervals. The green carpet glowed gently, and things were reflected in the polished floor and walls even more strongly than they were by day. Cat walked softly along, accompanied by several reflected ghosts of himself, until he hardly felt real. All the doors he saw were closed. Cat listened at one or two and heard nothing. He had not quite the courage to open any of them. He went on and on.

After a while, he found he had somehow worked round to the older part of the Castle. Here the walls were whitewashed stone, and all the windows went in nearly three feet before there was any glass. Then Cat came to a staircase which was the twin of the one that twisted up to his room, except that it twisted in the opposite direction. Cat went cautiously up it.

He was just on the last bend, when a door at the top opened. A brighter square of light shone on the wall at the head of the stairs, and a shadow stood in it that could only belong to Chrestomanci. No one else's shadow could be so tall, with such a smooth head and such a lot of ruffles on its shirt-front. Cat stopped.

'And let's hope the wretched girl won't try that again,' Chrestomanci said, out of sight above. He sounded a good deal more alert than usual, and rather angry.

Mr Saunders's voice, from further away, said, 'I've had about enough of her already, frankly. I suppose she'll come to her senses soon. What possessed her to give away the source of her power like that?'

'Ignorance,' said Chrestomanci. 'If I thought she had the least idea what she was doing, it would be the last thing she ever did in that line—or any other.'

'My back was to it,' said Mr Saunders. 'Which was it? Number five?'

'No. Number three by the look of its hair. A revenant,' said Chrestomanci. 'For which we must be thankful.' He began to come down the stairs. Cat was too scared to move. 'I'll have to get the Examining Board to revise their Elementary Magic Courses,' Chrestomanci called back as he came downstairs, 'to include more theory. These hedge-wizards push their good pupils straight on to advanced work without any proper grounding at all.' Saying this, Chrestomanci came down round the corner and saw Cat. 'Oh

107

hallo,' he said. 'I'd no idea you were here. Like to come up and have a look at Michael's workshop?'

Cat nodded. He did not dare do otherwise.

Chrestomanci seemed quite friendly, however, and so did Mr Saunders when Chrestomanci ushered Cat into the room at the top of the stairs. 'Hallo, Eric,' he said in his cheerful way. 'Have a look round. Does any of this mean anything to you?'

Cat shook his head. The room was round, like his own, but larger, and it was a regular magician's workshop. That much he could see. He recognised the five-pointed star painted on the floor. The smell coming from the burning cresset hanging from the ceiling was the same smell that had hung about Coven Street, back in Wolvercote. But he had no idea of the use of the things set out on the various trestle tables. One table was crowded with torts and limbecks, some bubbling, some empty. A second was piled with books and scrolls. The third bench had signs chalked all over it and a mummified creature of some sort lying among the signs.

Cat's eyes travelled over all this, and over more books crammed into shelves round the walls, and more shelves filled with jars of ingredients—big jars, like the ones in sweetshops. He realised Mr Saunders worked in a big way. His scudding eyes raced over some of the labels on the huge jars: *Newt's Eyes, Gum Arabic, Elixir St John's Wort, Dragon's Blood (dried).* This last jar was almost full of dark brown powder. Cat's eyes went back to the mummified animal stretched among the signs chalked on the third table. Its feet had claws like a dog's. It looked like a large lizard. But there seemed to be wings on its back. Cat was almost sure it had once been a small dragon.

'Means nothing, eh?' said Mr Saunders.

Cat turned round and found that Chrestomanci had gone. That made him a little easier. 'This must have cost a lot,' he said.

'The taxpayer pays, fortunately,' said Mr Saunders. 'Would you like to learn what all this is about?'

'You mean, learn witchcraft?' Cat asked. 'No. No thanks. I wouldn't be any good at it.'

'Well, I had at least two other things in mind besides witchcraft,' Mr Saunders said. 'But what makes you think you'd be no good?'

'Because I can't do it,' Cat explained. 'Spells just don't work for me.'

'Are you sure you went about them in the right way?' Mr Saunders asked. He wandered up to the mummified dragon—or whatever—and gave it an absent-minded flick. To Cat's disgust, the thing twitched all over. Filmy wings jerked and spread on its back. Then it went lifeless again. The sight sent Cat backing towards the door. He was almost as alarmed as he was the time Miss Larkins suddenly spoke with a man's voice. And, come to think of it, the voice had been not so unlike Mr Saunders's.

'I went about it every way I could think,' Cat said, backing. 'And I couldn't even turn buttons into gold. And that was simple.'

Mr Saunders laughed. 'Perhaps you weren't greedy enough. All right. Cut along, if you want to go.'

Cat fled, in great relief. As he ran through the strange corridors, he thought he ought to let Gwendolen know that Chrestomanci had, after all, been interested in her apparition, and even angry. But Gwendolen had locked her door and would not answer when he called to her.

*   *   *

He tried again next morning. But, before he had a chance to speak to Gwendolen, Euphemia came in, carrying a letter. As Gwendolen snatched it eagerly from Euphemia, Cat recognised Mr Nostrum's jagged writing on the envelope.

The next moment, Gwendolen was raging again. 'Who did this? When did this come?' The envelope had been neatly cut open along the top.

'This morning, by the postmark,' said Euphemia. 'And don't look at me like that. Miss Bessemer gave it to me open.'

'How *dare* she!' said Gwendolen. 'How dare she read my letters! I'm going straight to Chrestomanci about this!'

'You'll regret it if you do,' said Euphemia, as Gwendolen pushed past her to the door.

Gwendolen whirled round on her. 'Oh, shut up, you stupid frog-faced girl!' Cat thought that was a little unfair. Euphemia, though she did have rather goggling eyes, was actually quite pretty. 'Come on, Cat!' Gwendolen shouted at him, and she ran away along the corridor with her letter. Cat panted behind her and, once again, did not catch up with her until they were beside the marble staircase. 'Chrestomanci!' bawled Gwendolen, thin and small and unechoing.

Chrestomanci was coming up the marble staircase in a wide, flowing dressing-gown that was partly orange and partly bright pink. He looked like the Emperor of Peru. By the suave, vague look on his face, he had not noticed Gwendolen and Cat.

Gwendolen shouted down at him. 'Here, you! Come here at once!'

Chrestomanci's face turned upwards and his eyebrows went up. 'Someone's been opening my letters,' said Gwendolen. 'And I don't care who it is, but I'm not having it! Do you hear?'

Cat gasped at the way she spoke. Chrestomanci seemed perplexed. 'How are you not having it?' he said.

'I won't put up with it!' Gwendolen shouted at him. 'In future, my letters are going to come to me closed!'

'You mean you want me to steam them open and stick them down afterwards?' Chrestomanci asked doubtfully. 'It's more trouble, but I'll do that if it makes you happier.'

Gwendolen stared at him. 'You mean *you* did it? *You* read a letter addressed to *me*?'

Chrestomanci nodded blandly. 'Naturally. If someone like Henry Nostrum writes letters to you, I have to make sure he's not writing anything unsuitable. He's a very seedy person.'

'He was my teacher!' Gwendolen said furiously. 'You've no right to!'

'It's a pity,' said Chrestomanci, 'that you were taught by a hedge-wizard.

You'll have to unlearn such a lot. And it's a pity too that I've no right to open your letters. I hope you don't get many, or my conscience will give me no peace.'

'You intend to go on?' Gwendolen said. 'Then watch out. I warn you!'

'That is very considerate of you,' said Chrestomanci. 'I like to be warned.' He came up the rest of the marble stairs and went past Gwendolen and Cat. The pink and orange dressing-gown swirled, revealing a bright scarlet lining. Cat blinked.

Gwendolen stared vengefully as the dazzling dressing-gown flowed away along the gallery. 'Oh no, don't notice me, will you!' she said. 'Make jokes. You wait! Cat, I'm so furious!'

'You were awfully rude,' said Cat.

'He deserved it,' said Gwendolen, and began to hurry back towards the playroom. 'Opening poor Mr Nostrum's letter! It isn't that I mind him reading it. We arranged a code, so horrid Chrestomanci will never know what it's really saying, but there *is* the signature. But it's the insult. The indignity. I'm at their mercy in this Castle. I'm all on my own in distress and I can't even stop them reading my letters. But I'll show them. You wait!'

Cat knew better than to say anything. Gwendolen slammed into the playroom, flounced down at the table, and began at last to read her letter.

'I told you so,' said Euphemia, while Mary was working the lift.

Gwendolen shot her a look. 'You wait, too,' she said, and went on reading. After a bit, she looked in the envelope again. 'There's one for you too,' she said to Cat, and tossed him a sheet of paper. 'Mind you reply to it.'

Cat took it, wondering nervously why Mr Nostrum should write to him. But it was from Mrs Sharp. She wrote:

Me dear Cat,
Ow are you doin then me love? I fine meself lonesum an missin you both particular you the place seems so quiete. Thourght I was lookin forwards to a bit peace but missin yer voice an wishin you was comin in bringin appels. One thing happen an that was a gennelman come an give five poun for the ole cat that was

115

yer fidel so I feel flush an had idear of packin you up a parsel of jinjerbredmen and mebbe bringin them to you one of these days but Mr Nostrum sez not to. Spect your in the lap of luckshury anyhows. Love to Gwendolen. Wish you was back here Cat and the money means nothin.

Your loving,
Ellen Sharp

Cat read this with a warm, smiling, tearful feeling. He found he was missing Mrs Sharp as much as she evidently missed him. He was so homesick he could not eat his bread, and the cocoa seemed to choke him. He did not hear one word in five that Mr Saunders said.

'Is something the matter with you, Eric?' Mr Saunders demanded.

As Cat dragged his mind back from Coven Street, the window blacked out. The room was suddenly pitch dark. Julia squeaked. Mr Saunders groped his way to the switch and turned the light on. As he did so, the window became transparent again, revealing Roger grinning, Julia startled, Gwendolen sitting demurely, and Mr Saunders with his hand on the switch looking irritably at her.

'I suppose the cause of this is outside the Castle grounds, is it?' he said.

'Outside the lodge gates,' Gwendolen said smugly. 'I put it there this morning.' By this, Cat knew her campaign against Chrestomanci had been launched.

The window blacked out again.

'How often are we to expect this?' Mr Saunders said in the dark.

'Twice every half hour,' said Gwendolen.

'Thank you,' Mr Saunders said nastily, and he left the light on. 'Now we can see, Gwendolen, write out one hundred times, *I must keep the spirit of the law and not the letter* and, Roger, take that grin off your face.'

* * *

All that day, all the windows in the Castle blacked out regularly twice every half hour. But if Gwendolen had hoped to make Chrestomanci angry, she did not succeed. Nothing happened, except that everyone kept the lights on all the time. It was rather a nuisance, but no one seemed to mind.

Before lunch, Cat went outside on to the lawn to see what the blackouts looked like from the other side. It was rather as if two black shutters were flicking regularly across the rows of windows. They started at the top right-hand corner, and flicked steadily across, along the next row from left to right, and then from right to left along the next, and so on, until they reached the bottom. Then they started at the top again. Cat had watched about half a complete performance, when he found Roger beside him, watching critically with his pudgy hands in his pockets.

'Your sister must have a very tidy mind,' Roger said.

'I think all witches have,' said Cat. Then he was embarrassed. Of course he was talking to one—or at least to a warlock in the making.

'I don't seem to have,' Roger remarked, not in the least worried. 'Nor has Julia. And I don't think Michael has, really. Would you like to come and play in our tree-house after lessons?'

Cat was very flattered. He was so pleased that he forgot how homesick he was. He spent a very happy evening down in the wood, helping to rebuild the roof of the tree-house. He came back to the Castle when the dressing-gong went, and found that the window-spell was fading. When the windows darkened, it only produced a sort of grey twilight indoors. By the following morning, it was gone, and Chrestomanci had not said a word.

Gwendolen returned to the attack the next morning. She caught the baker's boy as he cycled through the lodge gates with the square front container of his bicycle piled high with loaves for the Castle. The baker's boy arrived at the kitchen looking a little dazed and saying his head felt swimmy. As a consequence, the children had to have scones for breakfast. It seemed that when the bread was cut, the most interesting things happened.

'You're giving us all a good laugh,' Mary said, as she brought the scones from the lift. 'I'll say that for your naughtiness, Gwendolen. Roberts thought he'd gone mad when he found he was cutting away at an old boot. So Cook cuts another, and next moment she and Nancy are trying to climb on the same chair because of all those white mice. But it was Mr Frazier's face that made me laugh most, when he says "Let me" and finds himself chipping at a stone. Then the—'

'Don't encourage her. You know what she's like,' said Euphemia.

'Be careful I don't start on you,' Gwendolen said sourly.

Roger found out privately from Mary what had happened to the other loaves. One had become a white rabbit, one had been an ostrich egg—which had burst tremendously all over the bootboy—and another a vast white onion. After that, Gwendolen's invention had run out and she had turned the rest into cheese. 'Old bad cheese, though,' Roger said, giving honour where honour was due.

It was not known whether Chrestomanci also gave honour where it was due, because, once again, he said not a word to anyone.

The next day was Saturday. Gwendolen caught the farmer delivering the churn of milk the Castle used daily. The breakfast cocoa tasted horrible.

'I'm beginning to get annoyed,' Julia said tartly. 'Daddy may take no notice, but he drinks tea with lemon.' She stared meaningly at Gwendolen. Gwendolen stared back, and there was that invisible feeling of clashing Cat had noticed when Gwendolen had wanted her mother's earrings from Mrs Sharp. This time, however, Gwendolen did not have things all her own way. She lowered her eyes and looked peevish.

'I'm getting sick of getting up early, anyway,' she said crossly.

This, from Gwendolen, simply meant she would do something later in the day in future. But Julia thought she had beaten Gwendolen, and this was a mistake.

They had lessons on Saturday morning, which annoyed Gwendolen very much. 'It's monstrous,' she said to Mr Saunders. 'Why do we have to be tormented like this?'

'It's the price I have to pay for my holiday on Wednesday,' Mr Saunders told her. 'And, speaking of tormenting, I prefer you to bewitch something other than the milk.'

'I'll remember that,' Gwendolen said sweetly.

CHAPTER SEVEN

It rained on Saturday afternoon. Gwendolen shut herself into her room, and once again Cat did not know what to do. He wrote to Mrs Sharp on the back of his postcard of the Castle, but that only took ten minutes, and it was too wet to go out and post it. Cat was hanging about at the foot of his stairs, wondering what to do now, when Roger came out of the playroom and saw him.

'Oh good,' said Roger. 'Julia won't play soldiers. Will you?'

'But I can't—not like you do,' Cat said.

'It doesn't matter,' said Roger. 'Honestly.'

122

But it did. No matter how cunningly Cat deployed his lifeless tin army, as soon as Roger's soldiers began to march, Cat's men fell over like ninepins. They fell in batches and droves and in battalions. Cat moved them furiously this way and that, grabbing them by handfuls and scooping them with the lid of the box, but he was always on the retreat. In five minutes, he was reduced to three soldiers hidden behind a cushion.

'This is no good,' said Roger.

'No, it isn't,' Cat agreed mournfully,.

'Julia,' said Roger.

'What?' said Julia. She was curled in the shabbiest armchair, managing to suck a lollipop, to read a book called *In the Hands of the Lamas*, and to knit, all at the same time. Her knitting, hardly surprisingly, looked like a vest for a giraffe which had been dipped in six shades of grey dye.

'Can you make Cat's soldiers move for him?' said Roger.

'I'm reading,' said Julia, round the edges of the lollipop. 'It's thrilling. One of them's got lost and they think he's

123

perished miserably.'

'Be a sport,' said Roger. 'I'll tell you whether he did perish, if you don't.'

'If you do, I'll turn your underpants to ice,' Julia said amiably. 'All right.' Without taking her eyes off her book or the lollipop out of her mouth, she fumbled out her handkerchief and tied a knot in it. She laid the knotted handkerchief on the arm of her chair and went on knitting.

Cat's fallen soldiers picked themselves up from the floor and straightened their tin tunics. This was a great improvement, though it was still not entirely satisfactory. Cat could not tell his soldiers what to do. He had to shoot them into position with his hands. The soldiers did not seem happy. They looked up at the great flapping hands above them in the greatest consternation. Cat was sure one fainted from terror. But he got them positioned in the end—with great cunning, he thought.

The battle began. The soldiers seemed to know how to do that for themselves. Cat had a company in

124

reserve behind a cushion and, when the battle was at its fiercest, he shooed them out to fall on Roger's right wing. Roger's right wing turned and fought. And every one of Cat's reserve turned and ran. The rest of his army saw them running away and ran too. In three seconds, they were all trying to hide in the toy-cupboard, and Roger's soldiers were cutting them down in swathes.

Roger was exasperated. 'Julia's soldiers *always* run away!'

'Because that's just what I would do,' Julia said, putting out a knitting-needle to mark her place in her book. 'I can't think why all soldiers don't.'

'Well, make them a bit braver,' said Roger. 'It's not fair on Eric.'

'You only said make them move,' Julia was arguing, when the door opened and Gwendolen put her head in.

'I want Cat,' she said.

'He's busy,' said Roger.

'That doesn't matter,' said Gwendolen. 'I need him.'

Julia stretched out a knitting-needle towards Gwendolen and wrote a little cross in the air with it. The cross floated, glowing, for a second. 'Out,' said Julia. 'Go away.' Gwendolen backed away from the cross and shut the door again. It was as if she could not help herself. The expression on her face was very annoyed indeed. Julia smiled placidly and pointed her knitting-needle towards Cat's soldiers. 'Carry on,' she said. 'I've filled their hearts with courage.'

*　　　*　　　*

When the dressing-gong sounded, Cat went to find out what Gwendolen had wanted him for. Gwendolen was very busy reading a fat, new-looking book and could not spare him any attention at first. Cat tipped his head sideways and read the title of the book. *Otherworld Studies, Series III*. While he was doing it, Gwendolen began to laugh. 'Oh, I see how it works now!' she exclaimed. 'It's even better than I thought! I know what to do now!' Then she lowered the book and asked Cat what he thought he was doing.

'Why did you need me?' said Cat. 'Where did you get that book?'

'From the Castle library,' said Gwendolen. 'And I don't need you now. I was going to explain to you about Mr Nostrum's plans, and I might even have told you about mine, but I changed my mind when you just sat there and let that fat prig Julia send me away.'

'I didn't know Mr Nostrum had any plans,' Cat said. 'The dressing-gong's gone.'

'Of course he has plans—and I heard it—why do you think I wrote to Chrestomanci?' said Gwendolen. 'But it's no good trying to wheedle me. I'm not going to tell you and you're going to be sorry. And piggy-priggy Julia is going to be sorrier even sooner!'

★   ★   ★

Gwendolen revenged herself on Julia at the start of dinner. A footman was just passing a bowl of soup over Julia's shoulder, when the skirt of Julia's dress turned to snakes. Julia jumped up with a shriek. Soup poured over the snakes and flew far and wide, and the footman yelled, 'Lord have mercy on us!' among the sounds of the smashing soup-bowl.

Then there was dead silence, except for the hissing of snakes. There were twenty of them, hanging by their tails from Julia's waistband, writhing and striking. Everyone froze, with their heads stiffly turned Julia's way. Julia stood like a statue, with her arms up out of reach of the snakes. She swallowed and said the words of a spell.

Nobody blamed her. Mr Saunders said, 'Good girl!'

Under the spell, the snakes stiffened and fanned out, so that they were standing like a ballet skirt above Julia's petticoats. Everyone could see where Julia had torn a flounce of a petticoat building the tree-house and mended it in a hurry with red darning wool.

'Have you been bitten?' said Chrestomanci.

'No,' said Julia. 'The soup muddled them. If you don't mind, I'll go and change this dress now.'

She left the room, walking very slowly and carefully, and Milly went with her. While the footmen, all rather green in the face, were clearing up the spilt soup,

Chrestomanci said, 'Spitefulness is one thing I won't have at the dinner-table. Gwendolen, oblige me by going to the playroom. Your food will be brought to you there.'

Gwendolen got up and went without a word. As Julia and Milly did not come back, the dining table seemed rather empty that evening. It was all stocks and shares from Bernard at one end, and statues again from Mr Saunders at the other.

★   ★   ★

Cat found that Gwendolen was rather triumphant. She felt she had made an impression on Chrestomanci at last. So she returned to the attack with a will on Sunday.

On Sunday, the Family dressed in its best and walked down to Morning Service at the village church. Witches are not supposed to like church. Nor are they supposed to be able to work magic there. But this never bothered Gwendolen at all. Mrs Sharp had many times remarked on it, as showing what exceptional talents Gwendolen had. Gwendolen sat next to Cat in the Chrestomanci pew, looking the picture of demure innocence in her broderie anglaise Sunday dress and hat, and found her place in her prayer book as if she were truly saintly.

The village people nudged one another and whispered about her. This rather pleased Gwendolen. She liked to be well-known. She kept up the pretence of saintliness until the sermon had begun.

The vicar climbed shakily into the pulpit and gave his text in a weak, wandering voice. 'For there were many in the congregation that were not sanctified.' This was certainly to the point. Unfortunately, nothing else he said was. He told, in his weak wandering voice, of weak wandering episodes in his early life. He compared them with weak wandering things he thought were happening in the world today. He told them they had better be sanctified or all sorts of things—which he forgot to mention—would happen, which reminded him of a weak wandering thing his aunts used to tell him.

Mr Saunders was asleep by this time, and so was stocks-and-shares Bernard. The old lady with mittens was nodding. One of the saints in the stained-glass windows yawned, and put up his crozier elegantly to cover his mouth. He looked round at his neighbour, who was a formidable nun. Her robes hung in severe folds, like a bundle of sticks. The bishop stretched out his stained-glass crozier and tapped the nun on the shoulder. She resented it. She marched into his window and began shaking him.

Cat saw her. He saw the coloured transparent bishop clouting the nun over the wimple, and the nun giving him as good as she got. Meanwhile, the hairy saint next to them made a dive for *his* neighbour, who was a kingly sort of saint, holding a model of the Castle. The kingly saint dropped his model and fled for protection, in a twinkle of glassy feet, behind the robes of a simpering lady saint. The hairy saint jumped gleefully up and down on the model of the Castle.

One by one, all the windows came to life. Almost every saint turned and

131

fought the one next to him. Those who had no one to fight, either hitched up their robes and did silly dances, or waved to the vicar, who rambled on without noticing. The little tiny people blowing trumpets in the corners of the windows sprang and gambolled and frisked, and pulled transparent faces at anyone who was looking. The hairy saint winkled the kingly one out from behind the simpering lady and chased him from window to window in and out of all the other fighting couples.

By this time, the whole congregation had seen. Everyone stared, or whispered, or leant craning this way and that to watch the twinkling glass toes of the kingly saint.

There was such a disturbance that Mr Saunders woke up, puzzled. He looked at the windows, understood, and looked sharply at Gwendolen. She sat with her eyes demurely cast down, the picture of innocence. Cat glanced at Chrestomanci. For all he could tell, Chrestomanci was attending to the vicar's every word and had not even noticed the windows. Milly was sitting on the edge of her seat, looking agitated. And the vicar still rambled on, quite unconscious of the turmoil.

The curate, however, felt he ought to put a stop to the unseemly behaviour of the windows. He fetched a cross and a candle. Followed by a giggling choirboy swinging incense, he went from window to window murmuring exorcisms. Gwendolen obligingly stopped each saint in its tracks as he came to it—which meant that the kingly saint was stranded halfway across the wall. But, as soon as the curate's back was turned, he began to run again, and the free-for-all went on more riotously than before. The congregation rolled about, gasping.

Chrestomanci turned and looked at Mr Saunders. Mr Saunders nodded. There was a sort of flicker, which jolted Cat where he sat, and, when he looked at the windows, every saint was standing stiff and glassy there, as they should be. Gwendolen's head came up indignantly. Then she shrugged. At the back of the church, a great stone crusader sat up on his tomb and, with much rasping of stone, thumbed his nose at the vicar.

'Dearly beloved—' said the vicar. He saw the crusader. He stopped, confounded.

The curate hastened up and tried to exorcise the crusader. A look of irritation crossed the crusader's face. He lifted his great stone sword. But Mr Saunders made a sharp gesture. The crusader, looking even more irritated, lowered his sword and lay down again with a thump that shook the church.

'There are some in this congregation who are certainly not sanctified,' the vicar said sadly. 'Let us pray.'

When everyone straggled out of church, Gwendolen sauntered out among them, quite impervious to the shocked looks everyone gave her as she passed. Milly hurried after her and seized her arm. She looked most upset. 'That was disgraceful, you ungodly child! I don't dare *speak* to the poor vicar. There is such a thing as going too far, you know!'

'Have I gone it?' Gwendolen asked, really interested.

'Very nearly,' said Milly.

But not quite, it seemed.

Chrestomanci did not say anything to Gwendolen, though he said a great deal, very soothingly, both to the vicar and to the curate.

'Why doesn't your father tell Gwendolen off?' Cat asked Roger as they walked back up the avenue. 'Taking no notice of her just makes her worse.'

'I don't know,' said Roger. 'He comes down on *us* hard enough if we use witchcraft. Perhaps he thinks she'll get tired of it. Has she told you what she's going to do tomorrow?' It was clear Roger could hardly wait.

'No. She's cross with me for playing soldiers with you,' said Cat.

'Her stupid fault for thinking she owns you,' said Roger. 'Let's get into old clothes and build some more of the tree-house.'

*　　　*　　　*

Gwendolen was angry when Cat went off with Roger again. Maybe that was why she thought of what she did next. Or perhaps, as she said, she had other reasons. At all events, when Cat woke up on Monday morning, it was dark. It felt very early. It looked even earlier. So Cat turned over and went to sleep again.

He was astonished to find Mary shaking him a minute later. 'It's twenty to nine, Eric. Get up, do!'

'But it's dark!' Cat protested. 'Is it raining?'

'No,' said Mary. 'Your sister's been hard at it again. And where she gets the strength from, a little girl like her, beats me!'

Feeling tired and Mondayish, Cat dragged himself out of bed and found he could not see out of the windows. Each window was a dark criss-cross of branches and leaves—green leaves, bluish cedar sprays, pine-needles, and leaves just turning yellow and brown. One window had a rose pressed against it, and there were bunches of grapes squashed on both of the others. And behind them, it looked as if there was a mile-thick forest. 'Good Lord!' he said.

'You may well look!' said Mary. 'That sister of yours has fetched every tree in the grounds and stood them as close as they can get to the Castle. You wonder

136

what she'll think of next.'

The darkness made Cat weary and gloomy. He did not want to get dressed. But Mary stood over him, and made him wash, too. The reason she was so dutiful, Cat suspected, was that she wanted to tell someone all about the difficulties the trees were causing. She told Cat that the yew trees from the formal garden were packed so tight by the kitchen door that the men had to hack a path for the milk to come through. There were three oak trees against the main front door, and no one could budge it. 'And the apples are all underfoot among the yew trees, so it smells like a cider-press in the kitchen,' Mary said.

When Cat arrived wearily in the playroom, it was even darker there. In the deep greenish light, he could see that Gwendolen was, understandably, white and tired. But she looked satisfied enough.

'I don't think I like these trees,' Cat whispered to her, when Roger and Julia had gone through to the schoolroom. 'Why couldn't you do something smaller

137

and funnier?'

'Because I'm not a laughing-stock!' Gwendolen hissed back. 'And I needed to do it. I had to know how much power I could draw on.'

'Quite a lot, I should think,' Cat said, looking at the mass of horse-chestnut leaves pressed against the window.

Gwendolen smiled. 'Better still when I've got my dragon's blood.'

Cat nearly blurted out that he had seen dragon's blood in Mr Saunders's workshop. But he stopped himself in time. He did not care for mighty works like this.

They spent another morning with the lights on, and at lunch time, Cat, Julia and Roger went out to have a look at the trees. They were disappointed to find that it was quite easy to get out of their private door. The rhododendrons were three feet away from it. Cat thought Gwendolen must intentionally have left them a way out, until he looked up and saw, from their bent branches and mashed leaves, that the bushes had indeed been squashed against the door earlier. It looked as if the trees were retreating.

Beyond the rhododendrons, they had to fight their way through something like a jungle. The trees were rammed so tight that, not only had twigs and leaves broken off by cartloads, but great branches had been torn away too, and fallen tangled with smashed roses, broken clematis and mangled grapes. When the children tore themselves out on the other side of the jungle, blank daylight hit them like a hammer blow. They blinked. The gardens, the village, and even the hills beyond were bald. The only place where they could still see trees was above the old grey ruined wall of Chrestomanci's garden.

'It must have been a strong spell,' said Roger.

'It's like a desert,' said Julia. 'I never thought I'd miss the trees so much!'

But, halfway through the afternoon, it became clear that the trees were going back to their proper places. They could see sky through the schoolroom window. A little later, the trees had spread out and retreated so much that Mr Saunders turned the light off.

Shortly after that, Cat and Roger noticed the ruins of the tree-house, smashed to bits in the crowding, dangling out of a chestnut tree.

'*Now* what are you staring at?' said Mr Saunders.

'The tree-house is broken,' Roger said, looking moodily at Gwendolen.

'Perhaps Gwendolen would be kind enough to mend it again,' Mr Saunders suggested sarcastically.

If he was trying to goad Gwendolen into doing a kindly act, he failed. Gwendolen tossed her head. 'Tree-houses are stupid babyish things,' she said coldly. She was very annoyed at the way the trees were retreating. 'It's too bad!' she told Cat just before dinner. By that time the trees were almost back to their usual places. The only ones nearer than they should be were those on the hill opposite. The view looked smaller, somehow. 'I hoped it would do for tomorrow, too,' Gwendolen said discontentedly. 'Now I shall have to think of something else.'

'Who sent them back? The garden warlocks?' Cat asked.

'I wish you wouldn't talk nonsense,' said Gwendolen. 'It's obvious who did it.'

'You mean Mr Saunders?' said Cat. 'But couldn't the spell have been used up just pulling all the trees here?'

'You don't know a thing about it,' said Gwendolen.

Cat knew he knew nothing of magic, but he found it queer all the same. The next day, when he went to see, there were no fallen twigs, torn-off branches or squashed grapes anywhere. The yew trees in the formal garden did not seem to have been hacked at all. And though there was not a trace of an apple underfoot round the kitchen, there were boxes of firm round apples in the courtyard. In the orchard, the apples were all either hanging on the trees or being picked and put in more boxes.

While Cat was finding this out, he had to flatten himself hastily against one of the hedge-like apple-trees to make way for a galloping Jersey cow pursued by two gardeners and a farm boy. There were cows galloping in the wood, when Cat went hopefully to look at the tree-

141

house. Alas, that was still a ruin. And the cows were doing their best to ruin the flowerbeds and not making much impression.

'Did you do the cows?' he asked Gwendolen.

'Yes. But it was just something to show them I'm not giving up,' said Gwendolen. 'I shall get my dragon's blood tomorrow and then I can do something really impressive.'

CHAPTER EIGHT

Gwendolen went down to the village to get her dragon's blood on Wednesday afternoon. She was in high glee. There were to be guests that night at the Castle and a big dinner party. Cat knew that everyone had carefully not mentioned it before, for fear Gwendolen would take advantage of it. But she had to be told on Wednesday morning, because there were special arrangements for the children. They were to have their supper in the playroom, and they were supposed to keep out of the way after that.

'I'll keep out of the way all right,' Gwendolen promised. 'But that won't make any difference.' She chuckled about it all the way to the village.

Cat was embarrassed when they got to the village. Everyone avoided Gwendolen. Mothers dragged their children indoors and snatched babies out of her way. Gwendolen hardly noticed. She was too intent on getting to Mr Baslam and getting her dragon's blood. Cat did not fancy Mr Baslam, or the decaying pickle smell among his stuffed animals. He let Gwendolen go there on her own, and went to post his postcard to Mrs Sharp in the sweet shop. The people there were rather cool with him, even though he spent nearly two shillings on sweets, and they were positively cold in the cake shop next door. When Cat came out on the green with his parcels, he found that children were being snatched out of his way, too.

This so shamed Cat that he fled back to the Castle grounds and did not wait for Gwendolen. There he wandered moodily, eating toffees and penny buns, and wishing he was back with Mrs Sharp. From time to time he saw Gwendolen in the distance. Sometimes she was dashing about. Sometimes she was squatting under a tree, carefully doing something. Cat did not go near her. If they were back with Mrs Sharp, he thought, Gwendolen would not need to do whatever impressive thing she was planning. He found himself wishing she was not quite such a strong and determined witch. He tried to imagine a Gwendolen who was not a witch, but he found himself quite unable to. She just would not be Gwendolen.

Indoors, the usual silence of the Castle was not quite the same. There were tense little noises, and the thrumming feeling of people diligently busy just out of earshot. Cat knew it was going to be a big, important dinner party.

After supper, he craned out of Gwendolen's window watching the guests come up the piece of avenue he could see from there. They came in carriages and in cars, all very large and rich-looking. One carriage was drawn by

144

six white horses and looked so impressive that Cat wondered if it might not even be the King.

'All the better,' said Gwendolen. She was squatting in the middle of the carpet, beside a sheet of paper. At one end of the paper was a bowl of ingredients. At the other crawled, wriggled or lay a horrid heap of things. Gwendolen had collected two frogs, an earthworm, several earwigs, a black beetle, a spider and a little pile of bones. The live things were charmed and could not move off the paper.

As soon as Cat was sure that there were no more carriages arriving, Gwendolen began pounding the ingredients together in the bowl. As she pounded, she muttered things in a groaning hum and her hair hung down and quivered over the bowl. Cat looked at the wriggling, hopping creatures and hoped that they were not going to be pounded up as ingredients too. It seemed not. Gwendolen at length sat back on her heels and said, 'Now!'

She snapped her fingers over the bowl. The ingredients caught fire, all by themselves, and burnt with small blue flames. 'It's working!' Gwendolen said excitedly. She snatched up a twist of newspaper from beside her and carefully untwisted it. 'Now for a pinch of dragon's blood.' She took a pinch of the dark brown powder and sprinkled it on the flames. There was a fizzing, and a thick smell of burning. Then the flames leapt up, a foot high, blazing a furious green and purple, colouring the whole room with dancing light.

Gwendolen's face glowed in the green and purple. She rocked on her heels, chanting, chanting, strings of things Cat could not understand. Then, still chanting, she leaned over and touched the spider. The spider grew. And grew. And grew more. It grew into a five foot monster—a greasy roundness with two little eyes on the front, hanging like a hammock amid eight bent and jointed furry legs. Gwendolen pointed. The door of her room sprang open of its own accord—which made her smile exultingly—and the huge spider went silently creeping towards it, swaying on its hairy legs. It squeezed its legs inwards to get through the door, and crept onwards, down the passage beyond.

Gwendolen touched the other creatures, one by one. The earwigs lumbered up and off, like shiny horned cows, bright brown and glistening. The frogs rose up, as big as men, and walked flap, flop on their enormous feet, with their arms trailing like gorillas. Their mottled skin quivered, and little holes in it kept opening and shutting. The puffy place under their chins made gulping movements. The black beetle crawled on branched legs, such a big black slab that it could barely get through the door. Cat could see it, and all the others, going in a slow, silent procession down the grass-green glowing corridor.

'Where are they going?' he whispered.

Gwendolen chuckled. 'I'm sending them to the dining room, of course. I don't think the guests will want much supper.'

She took up a bone next, and knocked each end of it sharply on the floor. As soon as she let go of it, it floated up into the air. There was a soft clattering, and more bones came out of nowhere to join it. The green and purple flames roared and rasped. A skull arrived last of all, and a complete skeleton was dangling there in front of the flames. Gwendolen smiled with satisfaction and took up another bone.

But bones when they are bewitched have a way of remembering who they were. The dangling skeleton sighed, in a hollow singing voice, 'Poor Sarah Jane. I'm poor Sarah Jane. Let me rest.'

Gwendolen waved it impatiently towards the door. It went dangling off, still sighing, and a second skeleton dangled after it, sighing, 'Bob the gardener's boy. I din't mean to do it.' They were followed by three more, each one singing softly and desolately of who it had been, and all five went slowly dangling after the black beetle. 'Sarah Jane,' Cat heard from the corridor. 'I din't mean to.' 'I was Duke of Buckingham once.'

Gwendolen took no notice of them and turned to the earthworm. It grew too. It grew into a massive pink thing as big as a sea serpent. Loops of it rose and fell and writhed all over the room. Cat was nearly sick. Its bare pink flesh had hairs on it like a pig's bristles. There were rings on it like the wrinkles round his own knuckles. Its great sightless front turned blindly this way and that until Gwendolen pointed to the door. Then it set off slowly after the skeletons, length after length of bare pink loops.

Gwendolen looked after it critically. 'Not bad,' she said. 'I need one last touch though.'

Carefully, she dropped another tiny pinch of dragon's blood on the flames. They burnt with a whistling sound, brighter, sicker, yellower. Gwendolen began to chant again, waving her arms this time. After a moment, a shape seemed to be gathering in the quivering air over the flames. Whiteness was boiling, moving, forming into a miserable bent thing with a big head. Three more somethings were roiling and hardening beneath it. When the first thing flopped out of the flames on to the carpet, Gwendolen gave a gurgle of pleasure. Cat was amazed at how wicked she looked.

'Oh don't!' he said. The three other somethings flopped on to the carpet, too, and he saw they were the apparition at the window and three others like it. The first was like a baby that was too small to walk—except that it *was* walking, with its big head wobbling. The next was a cripple, so twisted and cramped upon itself that it could barely hobble. The third was the apparition at the window, pitiful, wrinkled and draggled. The last had its white skin barred with blue stripes. All were weak and white and horrible. Cat shuddered all over.

'Please send them away!' he said.

Gwendolen only laughed again and waved the four apparitions towards the door.

They set off, toiling weakly. But they were only halfway there, when Chrestomanci came through the door and Mr Saunders came after him. In front of them came a shower of bones and small dead creatures pattering on to the carpet and getting squashed under Chrestomanci's long, shiny shoes. The apparitions hesitated, gibbering. Then they fled back to the flaming bowl and vanished. The flames vanished at the same time, into thick black smelly smoke.

Gwendolen stared at Chrestomanci and Mr Saunders through the smoke. Chrestomanci was magnificent in dark blue velvet, with lace ruffles at his wrists and on the front of his shirt. Mr Saunders seemed to have made an effort to find a suit that reached to the ends of his legs and arms, but had not quite succeeded. One of his big black patent-leather boots was unlaced, and there was a lot of shirt and wrist showing as he slowly coiled an invisible skein of something round his bony right hand. Both he and Chrestomanci looked back at Gwendolen most unpleasantly.

'You *were* warned, you know,' Chrestomanci said. 'Carry on, Michael.'

Mr Saunders put the invisible skein in his pocket. 'Thanks,' he said. 'I've been itching to for a week now.' He strode down on Gwendolen in a billow of black coat, yanked her to her feet, hauled her to a chair and put her face down over his knee. There he dragged off his unlaced big black boot and commenced spanking her with it hard and often.

While Mr Saunders laboured away, and Gwendolen screamed and squirmed and kicked, Chrestomanci marched up to Cat and boxed Cat's ears, twice on each side. Cat was so surprised that he would have fallen over, had not Chrestomanci hit the other side of his head each time and brought him upright again.

'What did you do that for?' Cat said indignantly, clutching both sides of his ringing face. 'I didn't do anything.'

'That's why I hit you,' said Chrestomanci. 'You didn't try to stop her, did you?' While Cat was gasping at the unfairness of this, he turned to the labouring Mr Saunders. 'I think that'll do now, Michael.'

Mr Saunders ceased swatting, rather regretfully. Gwendolen slid to her knees on the floor, sobbing with pain and making screams in between her sobs at being treated like this.

Chrestomanci went over and poked at her with his shiny foot. 'Stop it. Get up and behave yourself.' And, when

Gwendolen rose to her knees, staring piteously and looking utterly wronged, he said, 'You thoroughly deserved that spanking. And, as you probably realise, Michael has taken away your witchcraft, too. You're not a witch any longer. In future, you are not going to work one spell, unless you can prove to both of us that you are not going to do mischief with it. Is that clear? Now go to bed, and for goodness' sake try and think about what you've been doing.'

He nodded to Mr Saunders, and they both went out, Mr Saunders hopping because he was still putting his boot back on, and squashing the rest of the dead creatures as he hopped.

Gwendolen flopped forward on her face and drummed her toes on the carpet. 'The beast! The beasts! How dare they treat me like this! I shall do a worse thing than this now, and serve you all right!'

'But you can't do things without witchcraft,' Cat said. 'Was what Mr Saunders was winding up your witchcraft?'

'Go away!' Gwendolen screamed at

him. 'Leave me alone. You're as bad as the rest of them!' And, as Cat went to the door, leaving her drumming and sobbing, she raised her head and shouted after him, 'I'm not beaten yet! You'll see!'

*   *   *

Not surprisingly, Cat had bad dreams that night. They were terrible dreams, full of giant earthworms and great slimy, porous frogs. They became more and more feverish. Cat sweated and moaned and finally woke up, feeling wet and weak and rather too bony, the way you do when you have just had a bad illness or a fearsome dream. He lay for a little while feeling wretched. Then he began to feel better and fell asleep again.

*   *   *

When Cat woke again, it was light. He opened his eyes on the snowy silence of the Castle and was suddenly convinced that Gwendolen had done something else. He had no idea what made him so sure. He thought he was probably

154

imagining it. If Mr Saunders had truly taken Gwendolen's witchcraft away from her, she could not have done a thing. But he still knew she had.

He got up and padded to the windows to see what it was. But, for once, there was nothing abnormal about the view from any of them. The cedars spread above the lawn. The gardens blazed down the hill. The day was swimming in sun and mist, and not so much as a footprint marked the pearly grey-green of the grass. But Cat was still so sure that something, somewhere, was different that he got dressed and stole off downstairs to ask Gwendolen what she had done.

When Cat opened the door of her room, he could smell the sweet, charred, heavy smell that went with witchcraft. But that could have been left over from last night. The room was quite tidy. The dead creatures and the burnt bowl had been cleared away. The only thing out of place was Gwendolen's box, which had been pulled out of the painted wardrobe and stood with its lid half off near her bed.

Gwendolen was a sleeping hump under the blue velvet bedspread. Cat shut the door very gently behind him, in order not to disturb her. Gwendolen heard it. She sat up in bed with a bounce and stared at him.

As soon as she did, Cat knew that whatever was wrong, it was wrong with Gwendolen herself. She had her nightdress on back to front. The ribbons which usually tied it at the back were dangling at the front. That was the only thing obviously wrong. But there was something odd about the way Gwendolen was staring at him. She was astonished, and rather frightened.

'Who are you?' she said.

'I'm Cat, of course,' said Cat.

'No you're not. You're a boy,' said Gwendolen. 'Who are you?'

Cat realised that when witches lost their witchcraft, they also lost their memories. He saw he would have to be very patient with Gwendolen. 'I'm your brother, Eric,' he said patiently, and came across to the bed so that she could look at him. 'Only you always call me Cat.'

'My brother!' she exclaimed, in the greatest astonishment. 'Well, that can't be bad. I've always wanted a brother. And I know I can't be dreaming. It was too cold in the bath, and it hurts when I pinch myself. So would you mind telling me where I am? It's a Stately Home of some kind, isn't it?'

Cat stared at her. He began to suspect that her memory was perfectly good. It was not only the way she spoke and what she said. She was thinner than she should be. Her face was the right pretty face, with the right blue eyes, but the downright look on it was not right. The golden hair hanging over her shoulders was an inch longer than it had been last night.

'You're not Gwendolen!' he said.

'What a dreadful name!' said the girl in the bed. 'I should hope not! I'm Janet Chant.'

CHAPTER NINE

By this time, Cat was as bewildered as the strange girl seemed to be. Chant? he thought. Chant? Has Gwendolen a twin sister she hasn't told me about? 'But my name's Chant, too,' he said.

'Is it now?' said Janet. She knelt up in bed and scrubbed her hands thoughtfully about in her hair, in a way Gwendolen never would have done. 'Truly *Chant*? It's not that much of a common name. And you thought I was your sister? Well, I've put two and two together about a hundred times since I woke up in the bath, and I keep getting five. Where are we?'

'In Chrestomanci Castle,' said Cat. 'Chrestomanci had us to live here about a year after our parents died.'

'There you are!' said Janet. 'My Mum and Dad are alive and kicking—or they were when I said goodnight to them last night. Who's Chrestomanci? Could you just sketch your life history for me?'

Puzzled and uneasy, Cat described

how and why he and Gwendolen had come to live in the Castle, and what Gwendolen had done then.

'You mean Gwendolen really *was* a witch!' Janet exclaimed.

Cat wished she had not said *was*. He had a growing suspicion that he would never see the real Gwendolen again. 'Of course she is,' he said. 'Aren't you?'

'Great heavens no!' said Janet. 'Though I'm beginning to wonder if I mightn't have been, if I'd lived here all my life. Witches are quite common, are they?'

'And warlocks and necromancers,' said Cat. 'But wizards and magicians don't happen so often. I think Mr Saunders is a magician.'

'Medicine-men, witch-doctors, shamans, devils, enchanters?' Janet asked rapidly. 'Hags, fakirs, sorcerers? Are they thick on the ground too?'

'Most of those are for savages,' Cat explained. 'Hag is rude. But we have sorcerers and enchanters. Enchanters are very strong and important. I've never met one.'

'I see,' said Janet. She thought for a

159

moment and then swung herself out of bed, in a sort of scramble that was more like a boy's than a girl's, and again quite unlike the way Gwendolen would have done it. 'We'd better have a hunt round,' she said, 'in case dear Gwendolen has been kind enough to leave a message.'

'Don't call her that,' Cat said desolately. 'Where do you think she *is*?'

Janet looked at him and saw he was miserable. 'Sorry,' she said. 'I won't again. But you do see I might be a bit cross with her, don't you? She seems to have dumped me here and gone off somewhere. Let's hope she has a good explanation.'

'They spanked her with a boot and took away her magic,' Cat said.

'Yes, you said,' Janet replied, pulling open drawers in the golden dressing-table. 'I'm terrified of Chrestomanci already. But did they really take away her magic? How did she manage to do this, if they did?'

'I don't understand that either,' Cat said, joining in the search. By now, he would have given his little finger for a word from Gwendolen—any kind of word. He felt horribly lonely. 'Why were you in the bath?' he said, wondering whether to search the bathroom.

'I don't know. I just woke up there,' said Janet, shaking out a tangle of hair ribbons in the bottom drawer. 'I felt as if I'd been dragged through a hedge backwards, and I'd no clothes on, so I was freezing.'

'Why had you no clothes on?' Cat said, stirring Gwendolen's underclothes about, without success.

'I was hot in bed last night,' said Janet. 'So naked I came into this world. And I wandered about pinching myself—specially after I found this fabulous room. I thought I must have been turned into a princess. But there was this nightdress lying on the bed, so I put it on—'

'You've got it on back to front,' said Cat.

Janet stopped scanning the things on the mantelpiece to look down at the trailing ribbons. 'Have I? It won't be the only thing I'm going to get back to front,

161

by the sound of it. Try looking in that artistic wardrobe. Then I explored outside here, and all I found was miles of long green corridor, which gave me the creeps, and stately grounds out of the windows, so I came back in here and went to bed. I hoped that when I woke up it would all have gone away. And instead there was you. Found anything?'

'No,' said Cat. 'But there's her box—'

'It must be in there,' said Janet.

They squatted down and unpacked the box. There was not much in it. Cat knew that Gwendolen must have taken a lot of things with her to wherever she had gone. There were two books, *Elementary Spells* and *Magic for Beginners*, and some pages of notes on them. Janet looked at Gwendolen's large round writing.

'She writes just like I do. Why did she leave these books? Because they're First Form standard and she's up to O Levels, I suppose.' She put the books and notes to one side and, as she did so, the little red book of matches fell out from among them. Janet picked it up and opened it, and saw that half the matches were burnt

162

without having been torn out. 'That looks suspiciously like a spell to me,' she said. 'What are these bundles of letters?'

'My parents' love-letters, I think,' said Cat.

The letters were in their envelopes still, stamped and addressed. Janet squatted with a bundle in each hand. 'These stamps are penny blacks! No, it's a man's head on them. What's your King called?'

'Charles the Seventh,' said Cat.

'No Georges?' Janet asked. But she saw Cat was mystified and looked back at the letters again. 'Your mother and father were both called Chant, I see. Were they first cousins? Mine are. Granny didn't want them to marry, because it's supposed to be a bad thing.'

'I don't know. They may have been. They looked rather alike,' Cat said, and felt lonelier than ever.

Janet looked rather lonely too. She tucked the little book of matches carefully inside the pink tape that tied together the letters addressed to Miss Caroline Chant—like Gwendolen, she evidently had a tidy mind—and said,

'Both tall and fair, with blue eyes? My Mum's name is Caroline too. I'm beginning to see. Come on, Gwendolen, *give*!' And saying this, Janet tossed aside the letters and, in a most untidy way, scrabbled up the remaining folders, papers, writing-sets, pen-wipers and the bag with *Souvenir from Blackpool* on it. At the very bottom of the box was a large pink sheet of paper, covered all over with Gwendolen's best and roundest writing. 'Ah!' said Janet, pouncing on it. 'I thought so! She's got the same secretive mind as I have.' And she spread the letter on the carpet so that Cat could read it too. Gwendolen had written:

Dear Replacement,
I have to leave this terrible place. Nobody understands me. Nobody notices my talents. You will soon see because you are my exact double so you will be a witch too. I have been very clever. They do not know all my resauces. I have found out how to go to another world and I am going there for good. I know I shall be Queen of it because my fortune was

told and said so. There are hundreds of other worlds only some are nicer than others, they are formed when there is a big event in History like a battle or an earthquake when the result can be two or more quite diferent things. Both those things hapen but they cannot exist together so the world splits into two worlds witch start to go diferent after that. I know there must be Gwendolens in a lot of worlds but not how many. One of you will come here when I go because when I move it will make an empty space that will suck you in. Do not greive however if your parents still live. Some other Gwendolen will move into your place and pretend to be you because we are all so clever. You can carry on here making Chrestomanci's life a misery and I shall be greatful knowing it is in good hands.

Your loving
Gwendolen Chant

PS. Burn this.
PS2 Tell Cat I am quite sorry but he must *do what Mr Nostrum says.*

Having read this, Cat knelt wanly beside Janet, knowing he really would never see Gwendolen again. He seemed to be stuck with Janet instead. If you know a person as well as Cat knew Gwendolen, an exact double is hardly good enough. Janet was not a witch. The expressions on her face were nothing like the same. Looking at her now, Cat saw that, where Gwendolen would have been furious at being dragged into another world, Janet was looking as wan as he felt.

'I wonder how Mum and Dad are getting on with *my* Dear Replacement,' she said wryly. Then she pulled herself together. 'Do you mind if I don't burn this? It's the only proof I've got that I'm not Gwendolen who's suddenly gone mad and thinks she's this girl called Janet Chant. May I hide it?'

'It's your letter,' said Cat.

'And your sister,' said Janet. 'God bless her dear little sugar-coated shining soul! Don't get me wrong, Cat. I admire your sister. She thinks big. You have to admire her! All the same, I wonder if she's thought of the clever hiding-place where I'm going to put her letter. I shall feel better if she hasn't.'

Janet bounced up in her un-Gwendolenlike way and took the letter over to the gilded dressing-table. Cat bounced up and followed her. Janet took hold of the gold-garlanded mirror and swung it towards her on its swivels. The back was plain plywood. She dug her nails under the edge of the plywood and prised. It came free quite easily.

'I do this with my mirror at home,' Janet explained. 'It's a good hiding-place—it's about the one place my parents never think of. Mum and Dad are dears, but they're terribly nosy. I think it's because I'm their only one. And I like to be private. I write private stories for my eyes only, and they *will* try to read them. Oh, purple spotted dalmatians!'

She raised the wood up and showed Cat the signs painted on the red-coated back of the glass itself.

'Cabbala, I think,' said Cat. 'It's a spell.'

'So she did think of it!' said Janet. 'Really, it's hell having a double. You both get the same ideas. And working on that principle,' she said, sliding Gwendolen's letter between the plywood and the glass and pressing the plywood back in place, 'I bet I know what the spell's for. It's so Gwendolen can have a look from time to time and see how Dear Replacement's getting on. I hope she's looking now.' Janet swung the mirror back to its usual position and crossed her eyes at it, hideously. She took hold of the corners of her crossed eyes and pulled them long and Chinese, and stuck her tongue out as far as it would go. Then she pushed her nose up with one finger and twisted her mouth right round to one cheek. Cat could not help laughing. 'Can't Gwendolen do this?' Janet said out of the side of her face.

'No,' Cat giggled.

That was the moment when Euphemia opened the door. Janet jumped violently. She was much more nervous than Cat had realised. 'I'll thank you to stop pulling faces,' said Euphemia, 'and get out of your nightdress, Gwendolen.' She came into the room to make sure that Gwendolen did. She gave a croaking sort of shriek. Then she melted into a brown lump.

Janet's hands went over her mouth. She and Cat stared in horror as the brown lump that had been Euphemia grew smaller and smaller. When it was about three inches high, it stopped shrinking and put out large webbed feet. On these webbed feet, it crawled forward and stared at them reproachfully out of protruding yellowish eyes near the top of its head.

'Oh dear!' said Cat. It seemed that Gwendolen's last act had been to turn Euphemia into a frog.

Janet burst into tears. Cat was surprised. She had seemed so self-assured. Sobbing heavily, Janet knelt down and tenderly picked up the brown, crawling Euphemia. 'You poor girl!' she wept. 'I know just how you feel. Cat, what are we to do? How do you turn people back?'

'I don't know,' Cat said soberly. He was suddenly burdened with huge responsibilities. Janet, in spite of the confident way she talked, clearly needed looking after. Euphemia clearly needed it even more. If it had not been for Chrestomanci, Cat would have raced off to get Mr Saunders to help that moment. But he suddenly realised that if Chrestomanci ever found out what Gwendolen had done this time, the most terrible things would happen. Cat was quite sure of this. He discovered that he was terrified of Chrestomanci. He had been terrified of him all along, without realising it. He knew he would have to keep both Janet and Euphemia a secret somehow.

Feeling desperate, Cat raced to the bathroom, found a damp towel, and brought it to Janet. 'Put her down on this. She'll need to be wet. I'll ask Roger and Julia to turn her back. I'll tell them you won't. And for goodness sake don't tell anyone you aren't Gwendolen— please!'

Janet lowered Euphemia gently on to the towel. Euphemia scrambled round in it and continued to stare accusingly at Janet. 'Don't look like that. It wasn't me,' Janet said, sniffing. 'Cat, we'll have to hide her. Would she be comfortable in the wardrobe?'

'She'll have to be,' said Cat. 'You get dressed.'

A look of panic came over Janet's face. 'Cat, what does Gwendolen *wear*?'

Cat thought all girls knew what girls wore. 'The usual things—petticoats, stockings, dress, boots—you know.'

'No, I don't,' said Janet. 'I always wear trousers.'

Cat felt his problems mounting up. He hunted for clothes. Gwendolen seemed to have taken her best things with her, but he found her older boots, her green stockings and the garters to match, her second-best petticoats, her green cashmere dress with the smocking and—with some embarrassment—her knickers. 'There,' he said.

'Does she really wear two petticoats?' said Janet.

'Yes,' said Cat. 'Get them on.'

But Janet proved quite unable to get them on without his help. If he left her to do anything, she put it on back to front. He had to put her petticoats on her, button her up the back, tie her garters, fasten her boots, and put her dress on a second time, right way round, and tie its sash for her. When he had finished, it looked all right, but Janet had an odd air of being dressed up, rather than dressed. She looked at herself critically in the mirror. 'Thanks, you're an angel. I look rather like an Edwardian child. And I feel a right Charley.'

'Come on,' said Cat. 'Breakfast.' He carried Euphemia, croaking furiously, to the wardrobe and wrapped her firmly in the towel. 'Be quiet,' he told her. 'I'll get you changed back as soon as I can, so stop making that fuss, please!' He shut the door on her and wedged it with a page of Gwendolen's notes. Faint croaking came from behind it. Euphemia had no intention of being quiet. Cat did not really blame her.

'She's not happy in there,' Janet said, weakening. 'Can't she stay out in the room?'

'No,' said Cat. Frog though she was, Euphemia still looked like Euphemia. He knew Mary would recognise her as soon as she set eyes on her. He took Janet's resisting elbow and towed her along to the playroom.

'Don't you two ever get up till the last minute?' said Julia. 'I'm sick of waiting politely for breakfast.'

'Eric's been up for hours,' said Mary, hovering about. 'So I don't know what you've both been up to. Oh, what's Euphemia *doing*?'

'Mary's beside herself this morning,' Roger said. He winked. For a moment, there were two Marys, one real and one vague and ghostly. Janet jumped. It was only the second piece of witchcraft she had seen and she did not find it easy to get used to.

'I expect it's Gwendolen's fault,' said Julia, and she gave Janet one of those meaning stares.

Janet was very put out. Cat had forgotten to warn her how much Julia had disliked Gwendolen ever since the snakes. And a meaning stare from a witch is worse than a meaning stare from an ordinary person. Julia's pushed Janet backwards across the room, until Cat put himself in the way of it.

'Don't do that,' he said. 'She's sorry.'

'Is she?' said Julia. '*Are* you?' she asked, trying to get the stare round Cat to Janet again.

'Yes, horribly sorry,' Janet said fervently, not having the least idea why. 'I've had a complete change of heart.'

'I'll believe that when I see it,' said Julia. But she left off staring in order to watch Mary bringing the usual bread, the marmalade, and the jug of cocoa.

Janet looked, sniffed the cocoa steaming from the jug, and her face fell, rather like Gwendolen's on the first day. 'Oh dear. I hate cocoa,' she said.

Mary rolled her eyes to the ceiling. 'You and your airs and graces! You never said you hated it before.'

'I—I've had a revulsion of feeling,' Janet invented. 'When I had my change of heart, all my taste buds changed, too. I—you haven't any coffee, have you?'

'Where? Under the carpet or something?' Mary demanded. 'All right. I'll ask the kitchen. I'll tell them your taste buds are revolting, shall I?'

Cat was very pleased to hear that cocoa was not compulsory after all. 'Could I have coffee, too?' he asked, as Mary went to the lift. 'Or I prefer tea really.'

'But you waited to say so until Euphemia goes missing and leaves me all on my own!' Mary said, getting very put-upon.

'She never does anything anyway,' Cat said in surprise.

Mary flounced crossly to the speaking-tube and ordered a pot of coffee and a pot of tea. 'For Her Highness and His Nibs,' she said to it. '*He* seems to have caught it now. What wouldn't I give for a nice normal child in this place, Nancy!'

'But I *am* a nice normal child!' Janet and Cat protested in unison.

'And so are we—nice anyhow,' Julia said comfortably.

'How can you be normal?' Mary demanded as she let down the lift. 'All four of you are Chants. And when was a Chant ever normal? Answer me that.'

Janet looked questioningly at Cat, but Cat was as puzzled as she was. 'I thought your name was Chrestomanci,' he said to Roger and Julia.

'That's just Daddy's title,' said Julia.

'You're some kind of cousin of ours,' said Roger. 'Didn't you know? I always thought that was why Daddy had you to live here.'

As they started breakfast, Cat thought that this, if anything, made the situation more difficult than ever.

CHAPTER TEN

Cat watched his moment and, when Mr Saunders called them to lessons, he caught Roger's arm and whispered, 'Look, Gwendolen's turned Euphemia into a frog and—'

Roger gave a great snore of laughter. Cat had to wait for him to stop.

'And she won't turn her back. Can *you*?'

Roger tried to look serious, but laughter kept breaking through. 'I don't know. Probably not, unless she'll tell you what spell she used. Finding out which spell without knowing is Advanced Magic, and I'm not on that yet. Oh how funny!' He bent over the table and yelled with laughter.

Naturally, Mr Saunders appeared at

the door, remarking that the time for telling jokes was after lessons. They had to go through to the schoolroom. Naturally, Cat found Janet had sat in his desk by mistake. He got her out as quietly as he could and sat in it himself, distractedly wondering how he could find out which spell Gwendolen had used.

It was the most uncomfortable morning Cat had ever known. He had forgotten to tell Janet that the only thing Gwendolen knew about was witchcraft. Janet, as he had rather suspected, knew a lot, about a lot of things. But it all applied to her own world. About the only subject she would have been safe in was simple arithmetic. And Mr Saunders chose that morning to give her a History test. Cat, as he scratched away left-handed at an English essay, could see the panic growing on Janet's face.

'What do you mean, Henry V?' barked Mr Saunders. 'Richard II was on the throne until long after Agincourt. What was his greatest magical achievement?'

'Defeating the French,' Janet

guessed. Mr Saunders looked so exasperated that she babbled, 'Well, I think it was. He hampered the French with iron underwear, and the English wore wool, so they didn't stick in the mud, and probably their longbows were enchanted too. That would account for them not missing.'

'Who,' said Mr Saunders, 'do you imagine won the battle of Agincourt?'

'The English,' said Janet. This of course was true for her world, but the panic-stricken look on her face as she said it suggested that she suspected the opposite was true in this world. Which of course it was.

Mr Saunders put his hands to his head. 'No, no, no! The *French*! Don't you know *anything*, girl?'

Janet looked to be near tears. Cat was terrified. She was going to break down any second and tell Mr Saunders she was not Gwendolen. She did not have Cat's reasons for keeping quiet. 'Gwendolen never knows anything,' he remarked loudly, hoping Janet would take the hint. She did. She sighed with relief and relaxed.

'I'm aware of that,' said Mr Saunders. 'But somewhere, somewhere inside that marble head there must be a little cell of grey matter. So I keep looking.'

Unfortunately Janet, in her relief, became almost jolly. 'Would you like to take my head apart and look?' she asked.

'Don't tempt me!' cried Mr Saunders. He hid his eyes with one knobby hand and fended at Janet with the other. He looked so funny that Janet laughed. This was so unlike Gwendolen that Mr Saunders lowered his hand across his nose and stared at her suspiciously over it. 'What have you been up to now?'

'Nothing,' Janet said guiltily.

'Hm,' said Mr Saunders, in a way which made both Cat and Janet very uncomfortable.

At last—very long last—it was time for Mary to bring the milk and biscuits, which she did, with a very portentous look. Crouched on the tray beside Mr Saunders's cup of coffee was a large wet-looking brown thing. Cat's stomach seemed to leave him and take a plunge into the Castle cellars. From the look of Janet, hers was doing the same.

'What have you got there?' said Mr Saunders.

'Gwendolen's good deed for today,' Mary said grimly. 'It's Euphemia. Look at its face.'

Mr Saunders bent and looked. Then he whirled round on Janet so fiercely that Janet half got out of her seat. 'So that's what you were laughing about!'

'I didn't do it!' said Janet.

'Euphemia was in Gwendolen's room, shut in the wardrobe, croaking her poor head off,' said Mary.

'I think this calls for Chrestomanci,' Mr Saunders said. He strode towards the door.

The door opened before he got there and Chrestomanci himself came in, cheerful and busy, with some papers in one hand. 'Michael,' he said, 'have I caught you at the right—?' He stopped when he saw Mr Saunders's face. 'Is something wrong?'

'Will you please to look at this frog, sir,' said Mary. 'It was in Gwendolen's wardrobe.'

Chrestomanci was wearing an exquisite grey suit with faint lilac stripes

180

to it. He held his lilac silk cravat out of the way and bent to inspect the frog. Euphemia lifted her head and croaked at him beseechingly. There was a moment of ice-cold silence. It was a moment such as Cat hoped never to live through again. 'Bless my soul!' Chrestomanci said, gently as frost freezes a window. 'It's Eugenia.'

'Euphemia, Daddy,' said Julia.

'Euphemia,' said Chrestomanci. 'Of course. Now who did this?' Cat wondered how such a mild voice could send the hair pricking upright at the back of his head.

'Gwendolen, sir,' said Mary.

But Chrestomanci shook his smooth black head. 'No. Don't give a dog a bad name. It couldn't have been Gwendolen. Michael took her witchcraft away last night.'

'Oh,' said Mr Saunders, rather red in the face. 'Stupid of me!'

'So who could it have been?' Chrestomanci wondered.

There was another freezing silence. It seemed to Cat about as long as an Ice Age. During it, Julia began to smile. She drummed her fingers on her desk and looked meditatively at Janet. Janet saw her and jumped. She drew in her breath sharply. Cat panicked. He was sure Janet was going to say what Gwendolen had done. He said the only thing he could think of to stop her.

'I did it,' he said loudly.

Cat could hardly bear the way they all looked at him. Julia was disgusted, Roger astonished. Mr Saunders was fiercely angry. Mary looked at him as if he was a frog himself. But Chrestomanci was politely incredulous, and he was worst of all. 'I beg your pardon, Eric,' he said. 'This was *you*?'

Cat stared at him with a strange misty wetness round his eyes. He thought it was due to terror. 'It was a mistake,' he said. 'I was trying a spell. I—I didn't expect it to work. And then—and then Euphemia came in and turned into a frog. Just like that,' he explained.

Chrestomanci said, 'But you were told not to practise magic on your own.'

'I know.' Cat hung his head, without having to pretend. 'But I knew it wouldn't work. Only it did of course,' he explained.

'Well, you must undo the spell at once,' said Chrestomanci.

Cat swallowed. 'I can't. I don't know how to.'

Chrestomanci treated him to another look so polite, so scathing and so unbelieving, that Cat would gladly have crawled under his desk had he been able to move at all. 'Very well,' said Chrestomanci. 'Michael, perhaps you could oblige?'

Mary held the tray out. Mr Saunders took Euphemia and put her on the schoolroom table. Euphemia croaked agitatedly. 'Only a minute now,' Mr Saunders said soothingly. He held his hands cupped round her. Nothing happened. Looking a little puzzled, Mr Saunders began to mutter things. Still nothing happened. Euphemia's head bobbed anxiously above his bony fingers, and she was still a frog. Mr Saunders went from looking puzzled to looking baffled. 'This is a very strange spell,' he said. 'What did you use, Eric?'

'I can't remember,' said Cat.

'Well, it doesn't respond to anything I

can do,' said Mr Saunders. 'You'll have to do it, Eric. Come over here.'

Cat looked helplessly at Chrestomanci, but Chrestomanci nodded as if he thought Mr Saunders was quite right. Cat stood up. His legs had gone thick and weak, and his stomach seemed to have taken up permanent quarters in the Castle cellars. He slunk towards the table. When Euphemia saw him coming, she showed her opinion of the matter by taking a frantic leap off the edge of the table. Mr Saunders caught her in mid-air and put her back.

'What do I do?' Cat said, and his voice sounded like Euphemia croaking.

Mr Saunders took Cat by his left wrist and planted Cat's left hand on Euphemia's clammy back. 'Now take it off her,' he said.

'I—I—' said Cat. He supposed he ought to pretend to try. 'Stop being a frog and turn into Euphemia again,' he said, and wondered miserably what they would do to him when Euphemia didn't.

But, to his astonishment, Euphemia did. The frog turned warm under his fingers and burst into growth. Cat shot a look at Mr Saunders as the brown lump grew furiously larger and larger. He was almost sure he caught a secret smile on Mr Saunders's face. The next second, Euphemia was sitting on the edge of the table. Her clothes were a little crumpled and brown, but there was nothing else froggish about her. 'I never dreamt it was *you*!' she said to Cat. Then she put her face in her hands and cried.

Chrestomanci came up and put his arm round her. 'There, there, my dear. It must have been a terrible experience. I think you need to go and lie down.' And he took Euphemia out of the room.

'Phew!' said Janet.

Mary grimly handed out the milk and biscuits. Cat did not want his. His stomach had not yet come back from the cellars. Janet refused biscuits.

'I think the food here is awfully fattening,' she said unwisely. Julia took that as a personal insult. Her handkerchief came out and was knotted. Janet's glass of milk slipped through her fingers and smashed on the pitted floor.

'Clean it up,' said Mr Saunders.

'Then get out, you and Eric. I've had enough of both of you. Julia and Roger, get out magic text books, please.'

Cat took Janet out into the gardens. It seemed safest there. They wandered across the lawn, both rather limp after the morning's experiences.

'Cat,' said Janet, 'you're going to be very annoyed with me, but it's absolutely essential that I cling to you like a limpet all the time we're awake, until I know how to behave. You saved my bacon twice this morning. I thought I was going to die when she brought in that frog. Rigor mortis was setting in, and then you turned her back again! I didn't realise you were a witch too—no, it's a warlock, isn't it? Or are you a wizard?'

'I'm not,' said Cat. 'I'm not any of those things. Mr Saunders did it to give me a fright.'

'But Julia is a witch, isn't she?' said the shrewd Janet. 'What have I done to make her hate me so—or is it just general Gwendolenitis?'

Cat explained about the snakes.

'In which case I don't blame her,' said

186

Janet. 'But it's hard that she's in the schoolroom at the moment brushing up her witchcraft, and here I am without a rag of a spell to defend myself with. You don't know of a handy karate teacher, do you?'

'I never heard of one,' Cat said cautiously, wondering what karate might be.

'Oh well,' said Janet. 'Chrestomanci's a wonderfully fancy dresser, isn't he?'

Cat laughed. 'Wait till you see him in a dressing-gown!'

'I hardly can. It must be something! Why is he so terrifying?'

'He just is,' said Cat.

'Yes,' said Janet. 'He just is. When he saw the frog was Euphemia and went all mild and astonished like that, it froze the goose-pimples on my back. I *couldn't* have told him I wasn't Gwendolen—not even under the most refined modern tortures—and that's why I shall have to stick to you. Do you mind terribly?'

'Not at all,' said Cat. But he did rather. Janet could not have been more of a burden if she had been sitting on his shoulders with her legs wrapped round his chest. And to crown it all, it seemed as if there had been no need for his false confession. He took Janet to the ruins of the tree-house because he wanted something else to think about. Janet was enchanted with it. She swung herself up into the horse-chestnut to look at it, and Cat felt rather as you do when someone else gets into your railway carriage. 'Be careful,' he called crossly.

There was a strong rending noise up in the tree. 'Drat!' said Janet. 'These are ridiculous clothes for climbing trees in.'

'Can't you sew?' Cat called as he climbed up too.

'I despise it as female bondage,' said Janet. 'Yes, I can, actually. And I'm going to have to. It was both petticoats.' She tested the creaking floor that was all that remained of the house and stood up on it, trailing two different colours of frill below the hem of Gwendolen's dress. 'You can see into the village from here. There's a butcher's cart just turning in to the Castle drive.'

Cat climbed up beside her and they watched the cart and the dappled horse pulling it.

'Don't you have cars at all?' Janet asked. 'Everyone has cars in my world.'

'Rich people do,' said Cat. 'Chrestomanci sent his to meet us off the train.'

'And you have electric light,' said Janet. 'But everything else is old-fashioned compared with my world. I suppose people can get what they want by witchcraft. Do you have factories, or long-playing records, or high-rise blocks, or television, or aeroplanes at all?'

'I don't know what aeroplanes are,' said Cat. He had no idea what most of the other things were either, and he was bored with this talk.

Janet saw he was. She looked round for a change of subject and saw clusters of big green conker-cases hanging all round them at the ends of the branches. The leaves there were already singed-looking round the edges, suggesting that the conkers could not be far off ripe. Janet edged out along a branch and tried to reach the nearest cluster of green cases. They bobbed at the tips of her fingers, just out of reach. 'Oh dachshunds!' she said. 'They look almost ripe.'

'They aren't,' said Cat. 'But I wish they were.' He took a lathe out of the wreckage of the house and slashed at the conker-cases with it. He missed, but he must have shaken them. Eight or so dropped off the tree and went *plomp* on the ground below.

'Who says they're not ripe?' said Janet, leaning down.

Cat craned out of the tree and saw brown shiny conkers showing in the split green cases. 'Oh, hurray!' He came down the tree like a monkey, and Janet crashed after him, with her hair full of twigs. They scooped up the conkers greedily—wonderful conkers with grain on them like the contours in a map.

'A skewer!' Janet moaned. 'My kingdom for a skewer! We can thread them on my bootlaces.'

'Here's a skewer,' said Cat. There was one lying on the ground by his left hand. It must have fallen out of the tree-house.

They drilled conkers furiously. They took the laces out of Gwendolen's second-best boots. They discovered the rules of conkers were the same in both their worlds, and they went to the formal garden and held a battle royal there on the gravel path. As Janet firmly smashed Cat's last conker and yelled, 'Mine! Mine's a sevener now!' Milly came round a corner past a yew tree and stood laughing at them.

'Do you know, I wouldn't have thought the conkers were ripe yet. But it's been a lovely summer.'

Janet looked at her in consternation. She had no idea who this plump lady in the beautiful flowered silk dress could be.

'Hallo, *Milly*,' said Cat. Not that this helped Janet much.

Milly smiled and opened the handbag she was carrying. 'There are three things Gwendolen needs, I think. Here.' She handed Janet two safety-pins and a packet of bootlaces. 'I always believe in being prepared.'

'Th—thanks,' Janet stammered. She was horribly conscious of her gaping boots, her twig-filled hair and the two trailing strips of petticoat. She was even more confused by not knowing who

Milly was.

Cat knew that. He knew by now that Janet was one of those people who are not happy unless they have an explanation of everything. So he said fulsomely to Milly, 'I do think Roger and Julia are lucky, having a mother like you, Milly.'

Milly beamed and Janet looked enlightened. Cat felt dishonest. He *did* think that, but he would never have dreamt of saying it but for Janet.

Having gathered that Milly was Chrestomanci's wife, Janet was quite unable to resist going on and gathering as much more information as she could. 'Milly,' she said. 'Were Cat's parents first cousins like—I mean, were they? And what relation is Cat to you?'

'That sounds like those questions they ask you to find out how clever you are,' said Milly. 'And I don't know the answer, Gwendolen. It's my husband's family you're related to, you see, and I don't know too much about them. We need Chrestomanci here to explain, really.'

As it happened, Chrestomanci came

through the doorway in the garden wall at that moment. Milly rustled up to him, beaming.

'My love, we were needing you.'

Janet, who had her head down, trying to pin her petticoats, glanced up at Chrestomanci and then looked thoughtfully down at the path, as if the stones and sand there had suddenly become rather interesting.

'It's quite simple,' Chrestomanci said, when Milly had explained the question. 'Frank and Caroline Chant were my cousins—and first cousins to one another, too, of course. When they insisted on getting married, my family made a great fuss, and my uncles cut them off without a shilling in a thoroughly old-fashioned way. It is, you see, rather a bad thing for cousins to marry when there's witchcraft in the family. Not that cutting them off made the slightest difference, of course.' he smiled at Cat. He seemed thoroughly friendly. 'Does that answer the question?'

Cat had an inkling of how Gwendolen had felt. It was confusing and exasperating the way Chrestomanci would seem friendly when one ought to have been in disgrace. He could not resist asking, 'Is Euphemia all right?'

Then he wished he had not asked. Chrestomanci's smile snapped off like a light. 'Yes. She's feeling better now. You show touching concern, Eric. I believe you were so sorry for her that you hid her in a wardrobe?'

'My love, don't be so terrifying,' Milly said, hooking her arm through Chrestomanci's. 'It was an accident, and it's all over now.' She led him away down the path. But, just before they went out of sight behind a yew tree, Chrestomanci turned and looked over his shoulder at Cat and Janet. It was his bewildered look, but it was far from reassuring.

'Hot cross bunwrappers! Jiminy purple creepers!' Janet whispered. 'I'm beginning to hardly dare move in this place!' She finished pinning her petticoat. When Milly and Chrestomanci had had nearly a minute in which to walk out of hearing, she said, 'She's sweet—Milly—an absolute honey. But him! Cat, is it possible Chrestomanci is a rather powerful enchanter?'

'I don't think he is,' said Cat. 'Why?'

'Well,' said Janet, 'partly it's the feeling he gives—'

'I don't get a feeling,' said Cat. 'I'm just frightened of him.'

'That's *it*,' said Janet. 'You're probably muddled anyhow from having lived with witches all your life. But it isn't only a feeling. Have you noticed how he always comes when people call him? He's done it twice now.'

'Those were two complete accidents,' said Cat. 'You can't build ideas on accidents.'

'He disguises it quite well, I admit,' said Janet. 'He comes looking as if it was something else he was doing, but—'

'Oh do shut up! You're getting as bad as Gwendolen. She couldn't stop thinking of him for a moment,' Cat said crossly.

Janet pounded her open right boot on the gravel. 'I am *not* Gwendolen! I'm not even really *like* her! Get that into your fat head, will you!'

Cat started to laugh.

'Why are you laughing?' said Janet.

'Gwendolen always stamps when she's angry too,' said Cat.

'Gah!' said Janet.

CHAPTER ELEVEN

By the time Janet had laced both her boots, Cat was sure it was lunch-time. He hurried Janet back to the private door. They had nearly reached it, when a thick voice spoke among the rhododendrons.

'Young lady! Here a minute!'

Janet gave Cat an alarmed look and they both hurried for the door. It was not a pleasant voice. The rhododendrons clashed and rustled indignantly beside them. A fat old man in a dirty raincoat spilt out of them. Before they recovered from the surprise of seeing him, he had scuttled round between them and the door, where he stood looking at them reproachfully out of drooping red eyes and breathing beer-scented breath over them.

'Hallo, Mr Baslam,' Cat said, for Janet's benefit.

'Didn't you hear me, young lady?' Mr Baslam demanded.

Cat could see Janet was frightened of him, but she answered as coolly as Gwendolen might have done. 'Yes, but I thought it was the tree speaking.'

'The *tree* speaking!' said Mr Baslam. 'After all the trouble I been to for you, you take me for a tree! Three whole pints of bitter I had to buy that butcher to have him bring me in that cart of his, and I'm fair jolted to bits!'

'What do you want?' Janet said nervously.

'It's like this,' said Mr Baslam. He pulled aside his raincoat and searched slowly in the pockets of his loopy trousers.

'We have to go in for lunch,' said Cat.

'All in good time, young gentleman. Here we are,' said Mr Baslam. He held his pale grubby hand out towards Janet with two twinkling things in it. 'These.'

'Those are my mother's earrings!' Cat said, in surprise and for Janet's benefit.

'How did you get those?'

'Your sister give them me to pay for a little matter of some dragon's blood,' said Mr Baslam. 'And I dare say it was in good faith, young lady, but they're no good to me.'

'Why not?' asked Janet. 'They look like—I mean they're real diamonds.'

'True enough,' said Mr Baslam. 'But you never told me they was charmed, did you? They got a fearsome strong spell on them to stop them getting lost, these have. Terrible noisy spell. They was all night in the stuffed rabbit shouting out "I belong to Caroline Chant", and this morning I has to wrap them in a blanket before I dares take them to a man I know. And he wouldn't touch them. He said he wasn't going to risk anything shouting the name of Chant. So have them back, young lady. And you owe me fifty-five quid.'

Janet swallowed. So did Cat. 'I'm very sorry,' Janet said. 'I really had no idea. But—but I'm afraid I haven't any source of income at all. Couldn't you get the charm taken off?'

'And risk enquiries?' said Mr Baslam.

'That charm's deep in, I tell you.'

'Then why aren't they shouting now?' said Cat.

'What do you think I am?' said Mr Baslam. 'Could I sit in the joints of mutton shouting out I belonged to Miss Chant? No. This man I know obliges me with a bit of a spell on account. But he says to me, he says, "I can't only shut them up for an hour or so. That's a real strong charm. If you want it took off permanent, you'd have to take them to an enchanter. And that would cost you as much as the earrings are worth, besides getting questions asked." Enchanters are important people, young lady. So here I sits in them bushes, scared to death the spell's going to wear off before you comes by, and now you say you've no income! No—you have them back, young lady, and hand over a little something on account instead.'

Janet looked nervously at Cat. Cat sighed and felt in his pockets. All he had was half a crown. He offered it to Mr Baslam.

Mr Baslam backed away from it with a hurt, drooping look, like a whipped St

199

Bernard. 'Fifty-five quid I ask for, and you offer me half a crown! Son, are you having a joke on me?'

'It's all either of us has got,' said Cat, 'at the moment. But we each get a crown piece every week. If we give you that, we'll have paid you back in—' He did hurried calculations. Ten shillings a week, fifty-two weeks in a year, twenty-six pounds a year. 'It'll only take two years.' Two years was an appalling time to be without money. Still, Mr Baslam had got Gwendolen her dragon's blood, and it seemed fair that he should be paid.

But Mr Baslam looked more hurt than ever. He turned away from Cat and Janet and gazed mournfully up at the Castle walls. 'You live in a place like this, and tell me you can only get hold of ten bob a week! Don't play cruel games with me. You can lay your hands on no end of lucre if you puts your minds to it.'

'But we can't, honestly,' Cat protested.

'I think you should try, young gentleman,' said Mr Baslam. 'I'm not unreasonable. All I'm asking is twenty quid part-payment, interest of ten percent included, and the price of the shutting-up spell thrown in. That should come quite easy to you.'

'You know perfectly well it won't!' Janet said indignantly. 'You'd better keep those earrings. Your stuffed rabbit may look pretty in them.'

Mr Baslam gave her a very whipped look. At the same time, a thin, singing noise began to come from the palm of his hand where the earrings lay. It was too faint for Cat to pick up out the words, but it put paid to any notion that Mr Baslam had been lying. Mr Baslam's drooping look became less whipped. He looked more like a bloodhound hot on the trail. He let the earrings slide between his fat fingers and fall on the gravel.

'There they lie,' he said, 'if you care to stoop for them. I may remind you, young lady, that trade in dragon's blood is illicit, illegal and banned. I've obliged you in it. You've fobbed me off. Now I'm telling you that I need twenty quid by next Wednesday. That should give you time. If I don't get it, then Chrestomanci hears of the dragon's

201

blood Wednesday evening. And if he does, then I wouldn't be in your shoes, young lady, not for twenty thousand quid and a diamond tiara. Have I made myself clear?'

He had, appallingly. 'Suppose we give you the dragon's blood back?' Cat suggested desperately. Gwendolen had taken Mr Baslam's dragon's blood with her of course, but there was always that huge jar of it in Mr Saunders's workshop.

'What would I do with dragon's blood, son?' said Mr Baslam. 'I'm not a warlock. I'm only a poor supplier, and there's no demand for dragon's blood round here. It's the money I need. Twenty quid of it, by next Wednesday, and don't forget.' He gave them a bloodhound nod which flapped his eyes and his cheeks, and edged back into the rhododendrons. They heard him rustling stealthily away.

'What a nasty old man!' Janet said in a shaken whisper. 'I wish I really was Gwendolen. I'd turn him into a four-headed earwig. Ugh!' She bent and scrabbled the earrings up off the gravel.

Immediately, the air by the door was filled with high, singing voices. 'I belong to Caroline Chant! I belong to Caroline Chant!'

'Oh dear!' said Janet. 'They know.'

'Give them to me,' said Cat. 'Quick. Someone will hear.'

Janet poured the earrings into Cat's palm. The voices stopped at once. 'I can't get used to all this magic,' said Janet. 'Cat, what am I to do? How can I pay that horrible man?'

'There must be something we can sell,' said Cat. 'There's a junk shop in the village. Come on. We *must* get to lunch.'

They hurried up to the playroom, to find that Mary had already put plates of stew and dumplings in their places.

'Oh, look,' said Janet, who needed to relieve her feelings somehow. 'Nourishing fattening lunch. How nice!'

Mary glared at both of them and left the room without speaking. Julia's look was quite as unpleasant. As Janet sat down in front of her stew, Julia pulled her handkerchief out of her sleeve, already knotted, and laid it in her lap.

Janet put her fork into a dumpling. It stuck there. The dumpling was a white pebble, swimming with two others in a plateful of mud.

Janet carefully laid down her fork, with the pebble impaled on it, and put her knife neatly across the mud. She was trying to control herself, but, for a moment, she looked like Gwendolen at her most furious. 'I was quite hungry,' she said.

Julia smiled. 'What a pity,' she said cosily. 'And you've got no witchcraft to defend yourself with, have you?' She tied another smaller knot at the end of her handkerchief. 'You've got all sorts of things in your hair, Gwendolen,' she said as she pulled it tight. The twigs sticking in Janet's hair writhed and began dropping on the table and over her skirt. Each one was a large stripy caterpillar.

Janet was no more bothered by wriggly things than Gwendolen. She picked the caterpillars off and put them in a heap in front of Julia. 'I've a good mind to shout for your father,' she said.

'Oh, no, don't be a tell-tale,' said

204

Roger. 'Let her be, Julia.'

'Certainly not,' said Julia. 'She's not getting any lunch.'

After the meeting with Mr Baslam, Cat was not really very hungry. 'Here,' he said, and changed his plate of stew with Janet's mud. Janet started to protest. But, as soon as the plate of mud was in front of Cat, it was steaming stew again. And the looping heap of caterpillars was simply a pile of twigs.

Julia turned to Cat, not at all pleased. 'Don't you interfere. You annoy me. She treats you like a slave and all you do is stick up for her.'

'But I only changed the plates!' Cat said, puzzled. 'Why—?'

'It could have been Michael,' Roger suggested.

Julia glowered at him too. 'Was it you?' Roger blandly shook his head. Julia looked at him uncertainly. 'If I have to go without marmalade again,' she said at length, 'Gwendolen's going to know about it. And I hope the stew chokes you.'

★   ★   ★

205

Cat found it hard to concentrate on lessons that afternoon. He had to watch Janet like a hawk. Janet had decided that the only safe thing was to be totally stupid—she thought Gwendolen must have been pretty stupid anyway—and Cat knew she was overdoing it. Even Gwendolen had known the twice-times table. Cat was worried, too, in case Julia started knotting that handkerchief of hers when Mr Saunders's back was turned. Luckily, Julia did not quite dare. But Cat's main worry was how to find twenty pounds by next Wednesday. He could hardly bear to think of what might happen if he did not. The very least thing, he knew, would be Janet confessing she was not Gwendolen. He thought of Chrestomanci giving him that scathing stare and saying, '*You* went with Gwendolen to buy dragon's blood, Eric? But you knew it was illegal. And you tried to cover up by making Janet pretend to be Gwendolen? You show touching concern, Eric.' The mere idea made Cat shrivel up inside. But he had nothing to sell except a pair of earrings that shouted that they belonged to someone else. If he wrote to the Mayor of Wolvercote and asked if he could have twenty pounds out of the Fund, the Mayor would only write to Chrestomanci to ask why Cat wanted it. And then Chrestomanci would stare scathingly and say, '*You* went with Gwendolen to buy dragon's blood, Eric?' It was hopeless.

'Are you feeling well, Eric?' Mr Saunders asked several times.

'Oh, yes,' Cat replied each time. He was fairly sure that having your mind in three places at once did not count as illness, much as it felt like it.

'Play soldiers?' Roger suggested after lessons.

Cat would have liked to, but he dared not leave Janet on her own. 'I've got to do something,' he said.

'With Gwendolen. I know,' Roger said ·wearily. 'Anyone would think you were her left leg, or something.'

Cat felt hurt. The annoying thing was that he knew Janet could have done without her left leg more easily than she could have done without him. As he hurried after Janet to Gwendolen's room, he wished heartily it was really Gwendolen he was hurrying after.

Inside the room, Janet was feverishly collecting things: Gwendolen's spell books, the ornaments on the mantelpiece, the gold-backed brush and hand-mirror off the dressing-table, the jar on the bedside table, and half the towels from the bathroom.

'What are you doing?' said Cat.

'Finding things we can sell. Is there anything you can bear to spare from your room?' said Janet. 'Don't look like that. I know it amounts to stealing, but I get so desperate when I think of that horrible Mr Bisto going to Chrestomanci that I don't care any more.' She went to the wardrobe and rattled the clothes along the rail. 'There's an awfully good coat in here.'

'You'll need that on Sunday if it turns cold,' Cat said drearily. 'I'll go and see what I've got—only promise me to stay here until I come back.'

'Sho' ting,' said Janet. 'I daren't move widdout you, bwana. But hurry up.'

There were fewer things in Cat's

room, but he collected what he could find, and added the great sponge from the bathroom. He felt like a criminal. Janet and he wrapped their finds in two towels and crept downstairs with their chinking bundles, expecting someone to discover them any minute.

'I feel like a thief with the swag,' Janet whispered. 'Someone's going to shine a searchlight any second, and then the police will close in. *Are* there police here?'

'Yes,' said Cat. 'Do shut up.'

But, as usual, there was no one about near the private door. They crept down the shiny passage and peeped outside. The space by the rhododendrons was empty. They crept out towards them. Trees that would hide Mr Baslam would hide them and their loot.

They were three steps outside the door when a massed choir burst into song. Janet and Cat nearly jumped out of their skins. *'We belong to Chrestomanci Castle! We belong to Chrestomanci Castle!'* thundered forty voices. Some were deep, some were shrill, but all were very loud. They made a shattering noise.

209

It took them a second or so to realise that the voices were coming from their bundles.

'Creeping antimacassars!' said Janet.

They turned round and ran for the door again, with the forty voices bawling in their ears.

Miss Bessemer opened the door. She stood tall and narrow and purple, waiting for them to come through it. There was nothing Janet and Cat could do but scuttle guiltily past her into the passage, where they put their suddenly silent bundles down on the floor and steeled themselves for trouble.

'What an *awful* noise, my loves!' said Miss Bessemer. 'I haven't heard the like since a silly warlock tried to burgle us. What *were* you doing?'

Janet did not know who the stately purple lady was. She was too scared to speak. Cat had to say something. 'We were wanting to play houses in the tree-house,' he said. 'We needed some things for it.' He was surprised how likely he made it sound.

'You should have told me, sillies!' said Miss Bessemer. 'I could have given you some things that don't mind being taken outside. Run and put those back, and I'll look you out some nice furnishings for tomorrow.'

They crept dismally back to Janet's room. 'I just can't get used to the way everything's magic here,' Janet moaned. 'It's getting me down. Who was that long purple lady? I'm offering even money she's a sorceress.'

'Miss Bessemer. The housekeeper,' said Cat.

'Any hope that she'll give us splendid cast-offs that will fetch twenty quid in the open market?' Janet asked. They both knew that was unlikely. They were no nearer thinking of another way to earn twenty pounds when the dressing-gong went.

Cat had warned Janet what dinner was like. She had promised not to jump when footmen passed things over her shoulder, and sworn not to try and talk about statues with Mr Saunders. She assured Cat she would not mind hearing Bernard talk of stocks and shares. So Cat thought that for once he could be easy. He helped Janet dress and even had a shower himself, and when they went into the drawing room, he thought that they both did him credit.

But Mr Saunders proved at last to have worn out his craze for statues. Instead, everyone began to talk about identical twins, and then about exact doubles who were no relation. Even Bernard forgot to talk about shares in his interest in this new subject.

'The really difficult point,' he boomed, leaning forward with his eyebrows working up and down his forehead, 'is how such people fit in with a series of other worlds.'

And, to Cat's dismay, the talk turned to other worlds. He might have been interested at any other time. Now he dared not look at Janet, and could only wish that everyone would stop. But they talked eagerly, all of them, particularly Bernard and Mr Saunders. Cat learnt that a lot was known about other worlds. Numbers had been visited. Those which were best known had been divided into sets, called series, according to the events in History which were the same in them. It was very uncommon for people not to have at least one exact double in a world of the same series—usually people had a whole string of doubles, all along the set.

'But what about doubles outside a series?' Mr Saunders said. 'I have at least one double in Series III, and I suspect the existence of another in—'

Janet sat up sharply, gasping. 'Cat, help! It's like sitting on pins!'

Cat looked at Julia. He saw the little smile on her face, and the tail-end of her handkerchief above the table. 'Change places,' he whispered, feeling rather tired. He stood up. Everyone stared.

'All of which makes me feel that a satisfactory classification has not yet been found,' Mr Saunders said, as he turned Cat's way.

'Do you think,' said Cat, 'that I could change places with J-Gwendolen, please? She can't quite hear what Mr Saunders is saying from there.'

'Yes, and it's rivetingly interesting,' Janet gasped, shooting from her chair.

'If you find it essential,' Chrestomanci said, a little annoyed.

Cat sat in Janet's chair. He could feel

nothing wrong with it. Julia put her head down and gave him a long, unpleasant look, and her elbows worked as she crossly untied her handkerchief. Cat saw that she was going to hate him, too, now. He sighed. It was one thing after another.

Nevertheless, when Cat fell asleep that night, he was not feeling hopeless. He could not believe things could get any worse—so they had to get better. Perhaps Miss Bessemer would give them something very valuable, and they could sell it. Or, better still, perhaps Gwendolen would be back when he woke up, and already solving all his problems.

But when he went to Gwendolen's room in the morning, it was still Janet, struggling to tie her garters and saying over her shoulder, 'These things are probably very bad for people. Do you wear them, too? Or are they a female torture? And one *useful* thing magic could do would be to hold one's stockings up. It makes you think that witches can't be very practical.'

She did talk a lot, Cat thought. But it

was better than having no one in Gwendolen's place.

At breakfast, neither Mary nor Euphemia were at all friendly, and, as soon as they left the room, one of the curtains wrapped itself round Janet's neck and tried to strangle her. Cat took it away. It fought him like a live thing, because Julia was holding both ends of her handkerchief and pulling hard on the knot.

'Oh, do stop it, Julia!' he begged her.

'Yes, do,' Roger agreed. 'It's silly and it's boring. I need to enjoy my food in peace.'

'I'm quite willing to be friends,' Janet offered.

'That makes one of us,' said Julia. 'No.'

'Then be enemies!' Janet snapped, almost in Gwendolen's manner. 'I thought at first that you might be nice, but I can see now that you're just a tedious, pig-headed, cold-hearted, horny-handed, cross-eyed *hag*!'

That, of course, was calculated to make Julia adore her.

Luckily, Mr Saunders appeared

earlier than usual. There had only been time for Janet's marmalade to turn to orange worms, and change back again when Cat gave her his instead, and for Janet's coffee to become rich brown gravy, and turn to coffee again when Cat drank it, before Mr Saunders stuck his head round the door. At least, Cat thought it was lucky, until Mr Saunders said, 'Eric, Chrestomanci wants to see you now, in his study.'

Cat stood up. His stomach, full of charmed marmalade as it was, made an unusually rapid descent to the Castle cellars. Chrestomanci's found out, he thought. He knows about the dragon's blood and about Janet, and he's going to look at me politely and—Oh I do hope he *isn't* an enchanter!

'Where—where do I go?' he managed to say.

'Take him, Roger,' said Mr Saunders.

'And—and *why*?' Cat asked.

Mr Saunders smiled. 'You'll find out. Off you go.'

CHAPTER TWELVE

Chrestomanci's study was a large sun-filled room with books in shelves all round it. There was a desk, but Chrestomanci was not sitting at it. He was sprawled on a sofa in the sun, reading a newspaper and wearing a green dressing-gown with golden dragons on it. The gold embroidery of the dragons winked and glittered in the sun. Cat could not take his eyes off them. He stood just inside the door, not daring to go any further, and he thought: He *has* found out about the dragon's blood.

Chrestomanci looked up and smiled. 'Don't look so frightened,' he said, laying down his newspaper. 'Come and sit down.'

He pointed to a large leather armchair. It was all in his friendliest way, but, these days, Cat was sure this meant precisely nothing. He was sure that the friendlier Chrestomanci seemed, the angrier this meant he was. He stole over to the armchair and sat in it. It proved to be one of those deep, sloping kind of chairs. Cat slid backwards down the slippery leather slope of its seat until he found he was having to look at Chrestomanci from between his knees. He felt quite defenceless. He thought he ought to say something, so he whispered, 'Good morning.'

'You don't look as if you thought so,' observed Chrestomanci. 'No doubt you have your reasons. But don't worry. This isn't exactly about the frog again. You see, I've been thinking about you—'

'Oh, you needn't!' Cat said from his half-lying position. He felt that if Chrestomanci were to fix his thoughts on something on the other side of the universe, it would hardly be too far away.

'It didn't hurt much,' said Chrestomanci. 'Thank you all the same. As I was saying, the frog affair set me thinking. And though I fear you probably have as little moral sense as your wretched sister, I wondered if I could trust you. Do you think I can trust you?'

Cat had no idea where this could be leading, except that from the way Chrestomanci put it he did not seem to trust Cat very much. 'Nobody's ever trusted me before,' Cat said cautiously—except Janet, he thought, and only because she had no choice.

'But it might be worth trying, don't you think?' suggested Chrestomanci. 'I ask because I'm going to start you on witchcraft lessons.'

Cat had simply not expected this. He was horrified. His legs waved about in the chair with the shock. He managed to stop them, but he was still horrified. The moment Mr Saunders started trying to teach him magic, it would be obvious that Cat had no witchcraft at all. Then Chrestomanci would start to think about the frog all over again. Cat cursed the chance that had made Janet draw in her breath and caused him to confess. 'Oh you mustn't do that!' he said. 'It would be quite fatal. I mean, you can't trust me at all. I'm blackhearted. I'm evil. It was living with Mrs Sharp that did it. If I learnt witchcraft, there's no knowing what I'd do. Look what I did to

219

Euphemia.'

'That,' said Chrestomanci, 'is just the kind of accident I'm anxious to prevent. If you learn how and what to do, you're far less likely to make that kind of mistake again.'

'Yes, but I'd probably do it on purpose,' Cat assured him. 'You'll be putting the means in my hands.'

'You have it there anyway,' Chrestomanci said. 'And witchcraft will out, you know. No one who has it can resist using it for ever. What exactly makes you think you're so wicked?'

That question rather stumped Cat. 'I steal apples,' he said. 'And,' he suggested, 'I was quite keen on some of the things Gwendolen did.'

'Oh, me too,' Chrestomanci agreed. 'One wondered what she would think of next. How about her procession of nasties? Or those four apparitions?'

Cat shivered. He felt sick to think of them.

'Precisely,' said Chrestomanci, and to Cat's dismay, he smiled warmly at him. 'Right. We'll let Michael start you on elementary witchcraft on Monday.'

'Oh, *please* don't!' Cat struggled out of the slippery chair in order to plead better. 'I'll bring a plague of locusts. I'll be worse than Moses and Aaron.'

Chrestomanci said musingly, 'It might be quite useful if you parted the waters of the English Channel. Think of all the seasickness you'd save. Don't be so alarmed. We've no intention of teaching you to do things the way Gwendolen did.'

Cat trailed forlornly back to the schoolroom to find them having Geography. Mr Saunders was raging at Janet for not knowing where Atlantis was.

'How was I to know it's what I call America?' Janet asked Cat at lunchtime. 'Though, mind you, that was a lucky guess when I said it was ruled by the Incas. What's the matter, Cat? You look ready to cry. He's not found out about Mr Biswas, has he?'

'No, but it's quite as bad,' said Cat, and he explained.

'This was all we needed!' said Janet. 'Discovery threatens on all sides. But it may not be quite as bad as it seems, when I think. You might be able to work up a little magic if you practised first. Let's see what we can do after school with Gwendolen's books that the dear kind girl so obligingly left us.'

Cat was quite glad when lessons started again. He was sick of changing plates with Janet, and Julia's handkerchief must have been worn to rags with the number of knots tied in it. After lessons, he and Janet collected the two magic books and took them up to Cat's room. Janet looked round it with admiration.

'I like this room much better than mine. It's cheerful. Mine makes me feel like the Sleeping Beauty and Cinderella, and they were both such sickeningly sweet girls. Now let's get down to work. What's a really simple spell?'

They knelt on the floor, leafing through a book each. 'I wish I could find how to turn buttons into sovereigns,' said Cat. 'We could pay Mr Baslam then.'

'Don't talk about it,' said Janet. 'I'm at our wits' end. How about this? *Simple flotation exercise. Take a small mirror and lay it so that your face is visible in it. Keeping face visible, move round widdershins three times, twice silently willing, the third time saying: Rise little mirror, rise in air, rise to my head and then stay there. Mirror should then rise*—I think you ought to be able to manage that, Cat.'

'I'll have a go,' Cat said dubiously. 'What's widdershins?'

'Anti-clockwise,' said Janet. 'That I do know.'

'I thought it meant crawling,' Cat said humbly.

Janet looked at him consideringly. 'I suppose you're quite small still,' she said, 'but you do worry me when you go all cowed. Has anyone done anything to you?'

'I don't think so,' Cat said, rather surprised. 'Why?'

'Well, I never had a brother,' said Janet. 'Fetch a mirror.'

Cat got the hand-mirror from his chest of drawers and laid it carefully in the middle of the floor. 'Like that?'

Janet sighed. 'That's what I mean. I knew you'd get it if I ordered you to. Do you mind not being so kind and obedient? It makes me nervous. Anyway—' She took up the book. 'Can you see your face in it?'

'Almost nothing else,' said Cat.

'Funny. I can see *my* face,' said Janet. 'Can I do it, too?'

'You're more likely to get it to work than I am,' said Cat.

So they both circled the mirror, and they said the words in chorus. The door opened. Mary came in. Janet guiltily put the book behind her back.

'Yes, here he is,' Mary said. She stood aside to let a strange young man come into the room. 'This is Will Suggins,' she said. 'He's Euphemia's young man. He wants to talk to you, Eric.'

Will Suggins was tall and burly and rather handsome. His clothes looked as if he had brushed them carefully after working in a bakery all day. He was not friendly. 'It was you turned Euphemia into a frog, was it?' he said to Cat.

'Yes,' said Cat. He dared say nothing else with Mary there.

'You're rather small,' said Will Suggins. He seemed disappointed about

224

it. 'Anyway,' he said, 'whatever size you are, I'm not having Euphemia turned into things. I take exception to it. Understand?'

'I'm very sorry,' said Cat. 'I won't do it again.'

'Too right you won't!' said Will Suggins. 'You got off too light over this, by what Mary tells me. I'm going to teach you a lesson you won't forget in a hurry.'

'No, you're not!' said Janet. She marched up to Will Suggins and pushed *Magic for Beginners* threateningly towards him. 'You're three times his size, and he's said he's sorry. If you touch, Cat, I shall—' She took the book out of Will Suggins's chest in order to leaf hastily through it. 'I shall induce complete immobility in the legs and trunk.'

'And very pretty I shall look, I'm sure!' Will Suggins said, much amused. 'How are you going to do that without your witchcraft, may I ask? And if you did, I daresay I could get out of it fast enough. I'm a fair warlock myself. Though,' he said, turning to Mary, 'you might have warned me he was this small.'

'Not so small where witchcraft and mischief are concerned,' said Mary. 'Neither of them are. They're a pair of real bad lots.'

'Well, I'll do it by witchcraft then. I'm easy,' said Will Suggins. He searched in the pockets of his slightly floury jacket. 'Ah!' he said, and fetched out what seemed to be a lump of dough. For a moment he shaped it vigorously in both powerful hands. Then he rolled it into a ball and threw it at Cat's feet. It landed on the carpet with a soft *plop*. Cat looked at it in great apprehension, wondering what it was supposed to do.

'That'll lie there,' said Will Suggins, 'until three o'clock Sunday. Sunday's a bad time to be at witchcraft, but it's my free day. I shall be waiting for you then in Bedlam field, in the form of a tiger. I make a good tiger. You can turn yourself into something as large as you like, or small and fast if you prefer, and I'll teach you that lesson whatever you are. But if you don't come to Bedlam field in the form of something, that lump of dough

226

will start to work and you'll be a frog yourself—for as long as I feel like keeping you that way. Right, Mary. I'm through now.'

Will Suggins turned and marched out of the room. Mary followed him, but she was unable to resist putting her head back round the door to say, 'And see how you like that, Eric!' before she shut it.

Cat and Janet looked at one another and then at the lump of dough. 'What am I going to *do*?' said Cat.

Janet threw her book on to Cat's bed and tried to pick up the lump of dough. But it had grown to the carpet. She could not shift it. 'You'd only get this up by cutting a hole in the floor,' she said. 'Cat, this gets worse and worse. If you'll forgive my saying so, I've stopped loving your sugar-coated sister even one tiny bit!'

'It was my fault,' said Cat. 'I shouldn't have lied about Euphemia. That's what got me in this mess, not Gwendolen.'

'Mess is not a strong enough word,' said Janet. 'On Sunday, you get mauled by a tiger. On Monday, it comes out that you can't do magic. And if the whole story doesn't come out then, it will on Wednesday, when Mr Bedlam calls for his money. Do you think Fate has something up its sleeve for Tuesday too? I suppose if you go to meet him on Sunday in the form of yourself, he can't hurt you much, can he? It's better than waiting to be turned into a frog.'

'I'd better do that,' Cat agreed, looking at that ominous lump of dough. 'I wish I really could turn into things, though. I'd go as a flea. He'd scratch himself to bits trying to find me.'

Janet laughed. 'Let's see if there's a spell for it.' She turned round to fetch *Magic for Beginners* and hit her head on the mirror. It was hanging in the air, level with her forehead. 'Cat! One of us *did* it! Look!'

Cat looked, without much interest. He had too much else on his mind. 'I expect it was you. You're the same as Gwendolen, so you're bound to be able to work spells. But changing into things won't be in either of those books. That's Advanced Magic.'

'Then I'll do the spell to get the mirror

down,' said Janet. 'Not that I want to be a witch. The more I see of witchcraft, the more it seems just an easy way to be nasty.'

She had opened the book, when there was a knock at the door. Janet seized the chair beside Cat's bed and stood on it, so as to hide the mirror. Cat hastily dropped to one knee on top of the lump of dough. Neither of them wanted any more trouble.

Janet doubled *Magic for Beginners* inside out so that it could have been any book, and waved it at Cat. '*Come into the garden, Maud,*' she proclaimed.

Taking this as an invitation, Miss Bessemer opened the door and came in. She was carrying an armful of things, with a chipped teapot hanging off one finger. 'The furnishings I promised you, loves,' she said.

'Oh,' said Janet. 'Oh, thanks very much. We were just having a poetry reading, you know.'

'And I made sure you were talking to me!' Miss Bessemer said, laughing. 'My name's Maud. Will these be all right on the bed?'

'Yes, thanks,' said Cat.

Neither of them dared move. They twisted round to watch Miss Bessemer dump the armful on the bed, and, still twisted, they thanked her profusely. As soon as Miss Bessemer had gone, they dived to see if, by any blessed chance, any of the pile was valuable. Nothing was. As Janet said, if they really had wanted to play houses, two stools and an old carpet would have been just the thing, but from a selling point of view, they were just a dead loss.

'It was kind of her to remember,' Cat said, as he packed the heap into his cupboard.

'Except that now we'll have to remember to play houses with them,' Janet said morosely. 'As if we hadn't enough to do. Now, I *will* get this mirror down. I will!'

But the mirror refused to come down. Janet tried all three spells in both books, and it still stayed hanging in the air level with her head.

'You try, Cat,' said Janet. 'We can't leave it there.'

Cat roused himself from gloomily

230

staring at the ball of dough. It was still round. There was no sign that he had knelt on it, and that alarmed him. He knew it must be a very strong charm. But when Janet appealed to him, he sighed and reached up to pull the mirror down. His experience with Julia had taught him that a simple spell could usually be broken quite simply.

The mirror refused to descend an inch. But it slid about in the air. Cat was interested. He hung on to it with both hands, pushed off with his feet, and went travelling across the room in a most agreeable way.

'That looks fun,' said Janet.

'It is,' said Cat. 'You try.'

They played with the mirror for some time after that. It could go as fast as they could push it, and it took the weight of both of them easily. Janet discovered that the best ride was to be had by standing on the chest of drawers and jumping. Then, provided you kept your feet up, you could swing across the room and land on Cat's bed. They were whirling together across the carpet, tangled up and laughing a good deal, when Roger knocked at the door and came in.

'I say, that's a good idea!' he said. 'We've never thought of that. Can I have a go? And I met a peculiar cross-eyed man in the village, Gwendolen, and he gave me this letter for you.'

Cat dropped off on to the carpet and took the letter. It was from Mr Nostrum. Cat recognised the writing. He was so pleased that he said to Roger, 'Have twenty goes if you want!' and rushed up to Janet with the letter. 'Read it, quick! What does it say?'

Mr Nostrum could get them out of their troubles. He might not be much of a necromancer, but he was surely able to turn Cat into a flea, if Janet asked him nicely. He would certainly have a charm that could make Cat look as if he could do magic. And though Mr Nostrum was not rich, his brother William was. He could lend Cat twenty pounds, if he thought he was helping Gwendolen.

Cat sat on the bed beside Janet and they read the letter, while Roger trundled about the room dangling from the mirror and chuckling placidly at what fun it was. Mr Nostrum wrote:

My dear and favourite pupil,
I am here, domiciled at the White
Hart Inn. It is most important—I
repeat, of the utmost importance—that
you come to me here on Saturday
afternoon, bringing your brother to be
briefed by me.
Your affectionate and proud teacher,
Henry Nostrum.

At this, Janet looked nervous and mystified and moaned gently.

'I hope it's not bad news,' Roger said, sailing past with his feet hooked up behind him.

'No, it's the best news we could have had!' Cat said. He dug Janet in the ribs to make her smile. She smiled dutifully, but he could not make her see that it was good news, even when he had a chance to explain.

'If he taught Gwendolen, he'll know I'm not her,' she said. 'And if he doesn't know, he won't understand why you want to be turned into a flea. It is an odd thing to go and ask, even in this world.

233

And he'd want to know why I couldn't do it to you. Couldn't we tell him the truth?'

'No, because it's Gwendolen he's fond of,' Cat explained. Something told him that Mr Nostrum would be almost as little pleased as Chrestomanci to find that Gwendolen had departed for another world. 'And he's got some kind of plans for her.'

'Yes, this briefing,' Janet said irritably. 'He obviously thinks I know all about it. If you ask me, Cat, it's just one more damned thing!'

Nothing could convince Janet that salvation was at hand. Cat was quite sure it was. He went to sleep rejoicing, and woke up happy. He still felt happy, even when he trod on the lump of dough and it was cold and frog-like under his foot. He covered it up with *Magic for Beginners*. Then he had to turn his attention to the mirror. It would keep drifting out into the middle of the room. Cat had to tether it to the bookcase with his Sunday bootlace in the end.

He found Janet less happy than ever. Julia's latest idea was a mosquito. It met

Janet as she came into breakfast, and it kept with her, whining in and biting, all through lessons, until Cat swatted it with his arithmetic book. What with this, and nasty looks from both Julia and Mary, and then having to meet Mr Nostrum, Janet became both peevish and miserable.

'It's all right for you,' she said morbidly, as they tramped down the avenue on their way to the village that afternoon. 'You've been brought up with all this magic and you're used to it. But I'm not. And what scares me is that it's for ever. And it scares me even more that it *isn't* for ever. Suppose Gwendolen gets tired of her new world and decides to move on again? When that happens, off we shall be dragged, a whole string of us doubles, and I'll be having to cope in her world, and you'll have all your troubles over again with a new one.'

'Oh, I'm sure that won't happen,' Cat said, rather startled at the possibility. 'She's bound to come back soon.'

'Oh, *is* she?' said Janet. They came through the gates, and again mothers snatched children out of their sight, and

235

the village green emptied as they reached it. 'I *wish* I was back at home!' Janet wailed, almost in tears at the way everyone ran away.

CHAPTER THIRTEEN

They were ushered into a private parlour in the White Hart. Mr Henry Nostrum rolled pompously to meet them.

'My dear young friends!' He put his hands on Janet's shoulders and kissed her. Janet started backwards, knocking her hat over one ear. Cat was a little shaken. He had forgotten Mr Nostrum's seedy, shabby look, and the weird effect of his wandering left eye. 'Sit down, sit down!' said Mr Nostrum heartily. 'Have some ginger beer.'

They sat down. They sipped ginger beer, which neither of them liked. 'What did you want me for, as well as Gwendolen?' Cat asked.

'Because,' said Mr Nostrum, 'to come straight to the point and not to beat about the bush, we find, as we rather

236

feared we would, that we are quite unable to make use of those three signatures which you were kind enough to donate to me for services rendered in the tuition line. The Person Who Inhabits That Castle Yonder, whose name I disdain to say, signs his name under unbreakable protections. You may call it prudent of him. But I fear it necessitates our using Plan Two. Which was why, my dear Cat, we were so glad to arrange for you to live at the Castle.'

'What is Plan Two?' said Janet.

Mr Nostrum's odd eye slipped sideways across Janet's face. He did not seem to realise she was not Gwendolen. Perhaps his wandering eye did not see very well. 'Plan Two is just as I described it to you, my dear Gwendolen,' he said. 'We have not changed it one whit.'

Janet had to try another way to find out what he was talking about. She was getting quite good at it. 'I want you to describe it to Cat, though,' she said. 'He doesn't know about it, and he may need to because—because most unfortunately they've taken my witchcraft away.'

Mr Nostrum wagged a playful finger at her. 'Yes, naughty girl. I've been hearing things about you in the village. A sad thing to lose, but let us hope it will only be temporary. Now—as to explaining to young Cat—how shall I best go about it?' He thought, smoothing his frizzy wings of hair, as his habit was. Somehow, the way he did it showed Cat that whatever Mr Nostrum was going to tell him, it would not be quite the truth. It was in the movement of Mr Nostrum's hands, and in the very sit of his silver watch-chain his shabby, rounded waistcoat.

'Well, young Chant,' said Mr Nostrum, 'this is the matter in a nutshell. There is a group, a clique, a collection of people, headed by the Master of the Castle, who are behaving very selfishly in connection with witchcraft. They are keeping all the best things to themselves, which of course makes them very dangerous—a threat to all witches, and a looming disaster to ordinary people. For instance, take dragon's blood. You know that it is banned. These people, with That Person at their head, had it banned, and yet—mark this well, young Cat—they use it daily themselves. And—here is my point—they keep tight control of the ways to get to the worlds where dragon's blood comes from. An ordinary necromancer like myself can only get it at great risk and expense, and our exotic suppliers have to endanger themselves to get it for us. And the same goes for almost any product from another world.

'Now, I ask you, young Cat, is this fair? No. And I'll tell you why not, young Eric. It is not fair that the ways to other worlds should be in the hands of a few. That is the crux of the matter: the ways to other worlds. We want them opened up, made free to everyone. And that is where you come in, young Chant. The best and easiest way, the broadest Gateway to Elsewhere, if I may put it like that, is a certain enclosed garden in the grounds of this said Castle. I expect you have been forbidden to enter it—'

'Yes,' said Cat. 'We have been.'

'And consider how unfair!' said Mr Nostrum. 'The Master of That Place uses it every day and travels where he

239

pleases. So what I want you to do, young Cat, and this is all Plan Two amounts to, is to go into that garden at two-thirty precisely on Sunday afternoon. Can you promise me to do that?'

'What good would that do?' asked Cat.

'It would break the seal of enchantment these dastardly persons have set on the Gateways to Elsewhere,' Mr Nostrum said.

'I've never quite understood,' Janet said, with a very convincing wrinkle in her forehead, 'how Cat could break the seals just by going into the garden.'

Mr Nostrum looked a little irritated. 'By being an ordinary innocent lad, of course. My dear Gwendolen, I have stressed to you over and over again the importance of having an innocent lad at the centre of Plan Two. You *must* understand.'

'Oh, I do, I do,' Janet said hastily. 'And has it to be *this* Sunday at two-thirty?'

'As ever is,' said Mr Nostrum, smiling again. 'It's a good strong time. Will you do that for us, young Cat? Will you, by this simple act, set your sister and people like her free—free to do as they need in the practice of magic?'

'I'll get into trouble if I'm caught,' said Cat.

'A bit of boyish cunning will see you through. Then, never fear, we'll take care of you afterwards,' Mr Nostrum persuaded.

'I suppose I can try,' said Cat. 'But do you think you can help me a bit in return? Do you think your brother could very kindly lend us twenty pounds by next Wednesday?'

A vague, though affable, look affected Mr Nostrum's left eye. It pointed benevolently to the furthest corner of the parlour. 'Anything you please, dear boy. Just get into that garden, and the fruits of all the worlds will be yours for the picking.'

'I need to be a flea half an hour later, and I want to look as if I can do magic on Monday,' said Cat. 'That's all I need, apart from the twenty pounds.'

'Anything, anything! Just get into that garden for us,' said Mr Nostrum expansively.

241

With that, it seemed Cat and Janet had to be content. Cat made several efforts to fix Mr Nostrum in a definite promise, but all he would say was 'Just get into that garden'. Janet looked at Cat and they got up to go.

'Let us gossip,' suggested Mr Nostrum. 'I have at least two items of interest to you.'

'We haven't time,' Janet lied firmly. 'Come on, Cat.'

Mr Nostrum was used to Gwendolen being equally firm. He got up and led them to the Inn door like royalty and waved to them as they went out on to the green. 'I'll see you on Sunday,' he called after them.

'No you won't!' Janet whispered. Keeping her head down so that Gwendolen's broad hat hid her from Mr Nostrum, she whispered to Cat, 'Cat, if you do one thing that unbelievably dishonest man wants, you'll be a fool! I *know* he told you a pack of lies. I don't know what he's really after, but please don't do it.'

'I know—' Cat was beginning, when Mr Baslam got up from a bench outside the White Hart and shambled after them.

'Wait!' he puffed, rolling beer fumes over them. 'Young lady, young sir, I hope you're bearing in mind what I said to you. Wednesday. Don't forget Wednesday.'

'No fear. It haunts my dreams,' said Janet. 'Please. We're busy, Mr Bustle.'

They walked quickly away across the green. The only other living soul in sight was Will Suggins, who came out of the back yard of the bread shop in order to stare meaningly after them.

'I think I've *got* to do what he wants,' Cat said.

'Don't,' said Janet. 'Though I must say I can't see what else we can do.'

'About the only thing left is running away,' said Cat.

'Then let's do that—at once,' said Janet.

★   ★   ★

They did not exactly run. They walked briskly out of the village on the road Cat thought pointed nearest to Wolvercote.

243

When Janet objected that Wolvercote was the first place anyone at the Castle would think of looking, Cat explained about Mrs Sharp's grand contacts in London. He knew Mrs Sharp would smuggle them away somewhere, and no questions asked. He made himself very homesick by talking of Mrs Sharp. He missed her dreadfully. He trudged along the country road, wishing it was Coven Street and wishing Janet was not walking beside him making objections.

'Well, you may be right,' Janet said, 'and I don't know where else we could go. How do we get to Wolvercote? Hitch-hike?' When Cat did not understand, she explained that it meant getting lifts by waving your thumb.

'That would save a lot of walking,' Cat agreed.

The road he had chosen shortly turned into a very country lane, rutted and grassy and lined with high hedges hung with red briony berries. There was no traffic of any kind.

Janet managed not to point this out. 'One thing,' she said. 'If we're going to make a proper go of this, do promise me you won't happen to mention You Know Who.' When Cat did not understand this either, she explained, 'The man Mr Nostrum kept calling That Person and the Master of the Castle—you know!'

'Oh,' said Cat. 'You mean Chrest—'

'*Quiet!*' bawled Janet. 'I do mean him, and you mustn't say it. He's an enchanter and he comes when you call him, stupid! Just think of the way that Mr Nostrum was scared stiff to say his name.'

Cat thought about this. Gloomy and homesick as he was, he was not anxious to agree with anything Janet said. She was not really his sister, after all. Besides, Mr Nostrum had not been telling the truth. And Gwendolen had never said Chrestomanci was an enchanter. She would surely never have dared do all the magic she did if she thought he was. 'I don't believe you,' he said.

'All right. Don't,' said Janet. 'Just don't say his name.'

'I don't mind,' said Cat. 'I hope I never see him again anyway.'

The lane grew wilder as they walked.

It was a crisp warm afternoon. There were nuts in the hedges, and great bushes of blackberries. Before they had gone another half mile, Cat found his feelings had changed entirely. He was free. His troubles had been left behind. He and Janet picked the nuts, which were just ripe enough to eat, and laughed a good deal over cracking them. Janet took her hat off—as she told Cat repeatedly, she hated hats—and they filled the crown of it with blackberries for later on. They laughed when the juice oozed through the hat and dripped down Janet's dress.

'I think running away is fun,' said Cat.

'Wait till we're spending the night in a rat-infested barn,' said Janet. 'Flitterings and squeakings. Are there ghouls and goblins in this wor—? Oh look! There's a car coming! Thumb—no, wave. They probably don't understand thumbing.'

They waved furiously at the big black car that was whispering and bouncing along the ruts towards them. To their delight, it sighed to a stop beside them.

The nearest window rolled down. They got a very rude shock when Julia put her head out of it.

Julia was pale and agitated. 'Oh *please* come back!' she said. 'I know you ran away because of me, and I'm *sorry*! I swear I won't do it any more!'

Roger put his head out of the back window. 'I kept telling her you would,' he said. 'And she didn't believe me. Do come back. Please.'

The driver's door had opened by then. Milly came hurrying round the long bonnet of the car. She looked much more homely than usual, because her skirts were looped up for driving and she was wearing stout shoes and an old hat. She was as agitated as Julia. When she reached Janet and Cat, she flung an arm round each of them and hugged them so hard and thankfully that Cat nearly fell over.

'You poor darlings! Another time you get unhappy, you must come and tell me at *once*! And what a thing, too! I was so afraid you'd got into real trouble, and then Julia told me it was *her*. I'm extremely vexed with her. A girl did that

247

to me once and I know how miserable it made me. Now, please, please come back. I've got a surprise waiting for you at the Castle.'

There was nothing Cat and Janet could do but climb into the back of the car and be driven back to the Castle. They were miserable. Cat's misery was increased by the fact that he began to feel sick from the moment Milly started to bump the car backwards down the lane to a gate where she could turn it. The smell of blackberry coming from Janet's squashy hat made him feel worse.

Milly, Roger and Julia were very relieved to have found them. They chattered joyfully the whole way. Through his sickness, Cat got the impression that, although none of them said so, what they were particularly glad about was to have found Janet and Cat before Chrestomanci came to hear they were gone. This did not make either Cat or Janet feel any better.

In five minutes, the car had whispered up the avenue and stopped at the main door of the Castle. The butler opened it for them, just, Cat thought sadly, as

Gwendolen would have wished. The butler, furthermore, ceremoniously took Janet's leaking hat away from her. 'I'll see that these get to Cook,' he said.

Milly told Janet that her dress would just pass muster and hurried them to what was called the Little Drawing Room. 'Which means of course that it's a mere seventy feet square,' she said. 'Go in. Tea will be there for you.'

They went in. In the middle of the big square room, a wispy, skinny woman in beaded black clothes was sitting nervously on the edge of a gilded chair. She jumped round when the door opened.

Cat forgot he felt sick. 'Mrs Sharp!' he shouted, and ran to hug her.

Mrs Sharp was overjoyed, in spite of her nervousness. 'It's my Cat, then! Here, stand back, let me look at you, and you too, Gwendolen, love. My word, you do wear fine clothes to go playing about in! You're fatter, Cat. And Gwendolen, you've gone thin. I can understand that, dear, believe me! And would you just look at the tea they've brought for the three of us!'

It was a marvellous tea, even better than the tea on the lawn. Mrs Sharp, in her old greedy way, settled down to eat as much as she could, and to gossip hard. 'Yes, we came up on the train yesterday, Mr Nostrum and me. After I got your postcard, Cat, I couldn't rest till I'd had a look at you both, and seeing as how my contacts and other things have been paying nicely, I felt I owed it to myself. They treated me like royalty when I turned up here at the door, too. I can't fault them. But I wish I cared for it in this Castle. Tell me, Gwendolen, love, does it get you like it gets me?'

'How does it get you?' Janet asked cautiously.

'I'm nerves all over,' said Mrs Sharp. 'I feel weak and jumpy as a kitten—and that reminds me, Cat, but I'll tell you later. It's so *quiet* here. I kept trying to think what it was before you came—and you were a long time, my loves—and at last it came to me. It's an enchantment, that's what it is, a terrible strong one, too, against us witches. I said, "This Castle does not love witches, that's what it is!" and I felt for you, Gwendolen.

Make him send you to school away somewhere. You'd be happier.'

She chattered on. She was delighted to see them both, and she kept giving Cat particularly proud and affectionate looks. Cat thought she had convinced herself she had brought him up from a baby. After all, she had known him since he was born.

'Tell us about Coven Street,' he said yearningly.

'I was coming to that,' said Mrs Sharp. 'You remember Miss Larkins? Bad-tempered girl with red hair who used to tell fortunes? I never thought much to her myself. But someone did. She's been set up by a grateful client in a Salon in Bond Street. Coven Street's not good enough for her any more. The luck some people have! But I've had a stroke of luck myself, too. I told you in my letter—didn't I, Cat?—about being give five pounds for that old cat you turned our Cat's fiddle into, Gwendolen. Well, he was ever such a funny little man who bought him. While we were waiting to catch the old cat—you know how he never would come if you wanted him—

this little man kept at me, telling me all about stocks and shares and capital investment and such like. Things I never could understand. He told me what I ought to be doing with that five pound he was giving me, and making my head go round with it. Well, I didn't think too much of it, but I thought I'd have a go. And I did what he said, as far as I could remember. And do you know, that five pounds has brought in one hundred! One hundred pounds, he got me!'

'He must have been a financial wizard,' Janet said.

She meant it as a joke to cheer herself up. She needed cheering up for several reasons. But Mrs Sharp took her literally. 'He *was*, my dear! You're always so clever. I know he was, because I told Mr Nostrum, and Mr Nostrum did exactly what I did with five pounds of his own—or it may have been more— and he lost every penny of it. And another thing—'

Cat watched Mrs Sharp as she chattered on. He was puzzled and sad. He was still just as fond of Mrs Sharp.

But he knew it would have been no use whatsoever running away to her. She was a weak, dishonest person. She would not have helped them. She would have sent them back to the Castle and tried to get money out of Chrestomanci for doing it. And the London contacts she was boasting of at that moment were just boasts. Cat wondered how much he had changed inside—and why he had—enough to know all this. But he did know, just as surely as if Mrs Sharp had turned round in her gilded chair and assured him of it herself, and it upset him.

As Mrs Sharp came to the end of the food, she seemed to become very nervous. Perhaps the Castle was getting her down. At length she got up and took a nervous trot to the distant window, absent-mindedly taking her teacup with her.

'Come and explain this view,' she called. 'It's so grand I can't understand it.' Cat and Janet obligingly went over to her. Whereupon Mrs Sharp became astounded to find she had an empty teacup in her hand. 'Oh, look at this,' she said, shaking with nervousness. 'I'll be carrying it away with me if I'm not careful.'

'You'd better not,' said Cat. 'It's bound to be charmed. Everything you take outside shouts where it came from.'

'Is that so?' All of a flutter, Mrs Sharp passed Janet her cup and followed it up, very guiltily, with two silver spoons and the sugar-tongs out of her handbag. 'There, dear. Would you mind taking those back to the table?' Janet set off across the yards of carpet and, as soon as she was out of hearing, Mrs Sharp bent and whispered, 'Have you talked to Mr Nostrum, Cat?'

Cat nodded.

Mrs Sharp at once became nervous in a much more genuine way. 'Don't do what he says, love,' she whispered. 'Not on *any* account. You hear me? It's a wicked, crying shame, and you're not to do it!' Then, as Janet came slowly back—slowly, because she could see Mrs Sharp had something private to say to Cat—Mrs Sharp burst out artificially, 'Oh those great immemorial oaks! They must be older than I am!'

'They're cedars,' was all Cat could think of to say.

'Well, that was a nice tea, my loves, and lovely to see you,' said Mrs Sharp. 'And I'm glad you warned me about those spoons. It's a mean, wicked trick enchanting property, I always think. I must be going now. Mr Nostrum's expecting me.' And go Mrs Sharp did, through the Castle hall and away down the avenue with such speed that it was clear she was glad to go.

'You can see the Castle really upsets her,' Janet said, watching Mrs Sharp's trotting black figure. 'There is this quiet. I know what she means. But I think it's cheerful—or it would be if everything else wasn't so miserable. Cat, it would have been no good running away to her, I'm afraid.'

'I know,' said Cat.

'I thought you did,' said Janet.

She was wanting to say more, but they were interrupted by Roger and Julia. Julia was so contrite and trying so hard to be friendly that neither Janet nor Cat had the heart to go off on their own. They played with hand-mirrors instead.

Roger fetched the mirror tethered to Cat's bookcase, and collected his own and Julia's and Gwendolen's too. Julia took a firm little reef in that handkerchief of hers and sent all four aloft in the playroom. Until supper, they had great fun whizzing round the playroom, not to speak of up and down the passage outside.

*   *   *

Supper was in the playroom that evening. There were guests to dinner again downstairs. Roger and Julia knew, but no one had mentioned it to Cat and Janet for fear the supposed Gwendolen might try to ruin it again.

'They always entertain a lot in the month before Hallowe'en,' Julia said as they finished the blackberry tart Cook had made specially out of Janet's hatful. 'Shall we play soldiers now, or mirrors again?'

Janet was signalling so hard that she had something urgent to say, that Cat had to refuse. 'I'm awfully sorry. We've got to talk about something Mrs Sharp told us. And don't say Gwendolen owns me. It's not that at all.'

'We forgive you,' Roger said. 'We might forgive Gwendolen too, with luck.'

'We'll come back when I've said it,' said Janet.

They hurried along to her room, and Janet locked the door in case Euphemia tried to come in.

'Mrs Sharp said I wasn't on any account to do what Mr Nostrum says,' Cat told her. 'I think she came specially to tell me.'

'Yes, she's fond of you,' said Janet. 'Oh—oh—oh *drat*!' She clasped her hands behind her back and marched up and down with her head bent. She looked so like Mr Saunders teaching, that Cat started to laugh. 'Bother,' said Janet. 'Bother, bother, bother bother botherbotherbother!' She marched some more. 'Mrs Sharp is a highly dishonest person, almost as bad as Mr Nostrum, and probably worse than Mr Bistro, so if *she* thinks you oughtn't to do it, it must be bad. What are you laughing about?'

'You keep getting Mr Baslam's name wrong,' said Cat.

'He doesn't deserve to have it got right,' Janet said, marching on. 'Oh, confusticate Mrs Sharp! After I saw she wasn't any good for any kind of help, I was in such despair that I suddenly saw the ideal way out—and she's stopped it. You see, if that garden is a way to go to other worlds, you and I could go back to my world, and you could live there with me. Don't you think that was a good idea? You'd be safe from Chrestomanci and Mr Baalamb, and I'm sure Will Suggins couldn't turn you into a frog there, either, could he?'

'No,' Cat said dubiously. 'But I don't think Mr Nostrum was telling quite the truth. All sort of things could be wrong.'

'Don't I know it!' said Janet. 'Specially after Mrs Sharp. Mum and Dad would be another difficulty too— though I'm sure they'd like you when they understood. They must be fearfully puzzled by my Dear Replacement by now, as it is. And I did have a brother, who died when he was born, so perhaps they'd think you were *his* Dear

Replacement.'

'That's funny!' said Cat. 'I nearly died being born too.'

'Then you must be him,' said Janet, swinging round at the end of her march. 'They'd be delighted—I hope. And the best of it would have been that Gwendolen would have been dragged back here to face the music—and serve her right! This is all her fault.'

'No, it isn't,' said Cat.

'Yes, it *is*!' said Janet. 'She did magic when she was forbidden to, and gave Mr Blastoff dud earrings for something she wasn't supposed to have anyway, and dragged me here, and turned Euphemia into a frog, and got you into an even worse mess than I'm in. Will you stop being so loyal for a moment and *notice*!'

'It's no good getting angry,' said Cat, and he sighed. He missed Gwendolen even more than he had missed Mrs Sharp.

Janet sighed too, but with exasperation. She sat down at the dressing-table with a thump and stared into her own cross face. She pushed its nose up and crossed her eyes. She had been doing this every spare minute. It relieved her feelings about Gwendolen a little.

Cat had been thinking. 'I think it's a good idea,' he said dolefully. 'We'd better go to the garden. But I think you need some kind of magic to go to another world.'

'Thus we find ourselves stumped,' said Janet. 'It's dangerous, and we can't anyway. But they'd taken Gwendolen's witchcraft away, and *she* did it. How? That's been puzzling me a lot.'

'I expect she used dragon's blood,' said Cat. 'She still had that. Mr Saunders has a whole jar of dragon's blood up in his workshop.'

'Why didn't you *say* so?' Janet yelled, jumping round on her stool.

She really might have been Gwendolen. At the sight of her fierce face Cat missed Gwendolen more than ever. He resented Janet. She had been ordering him about all day. Then she tried to make out it was all Gwendolen's fault. He shrugged mulishly and went very unhelpful. 'You didn't ask.'

'But can you get some?'

'Maybe. But,' Cat added, 'I don't want to go to another world really.'

Janet drew a long, quiet breath and managed not to tell him to stay and be turned into a frog then. She made a very ingenious face at the mirror and counted up to ten. 'Cat,' she said carefully, 'we really are in such a mess here that I can't see any other way out. Can you?'

'No,' Cat admitted grudgingly. 'I said I'd go.'

'And thank you, dear Janet, for your kind invitation, I notice,' Janet said. To her relief, Cat grinned. 'But we'll have to be hideously careful about going,' she said, 'because I suspect that if Chrestomanci doesn't know what we're doing, Milly will.'

'Milly?' said Cat.

'Milly,' said Janet. 'I think she's a witch.' She ducked her head down and fiddled with the gold-backed hairbrush. 'I know you think I go around seeing sorcery everywhere with my nasty suspicious mind, like you did about Chrestomanci, but I really am sure, Cat. A sweet, kind honey of a witch if you like. But she *is* one. How else did she

261

know we were running away this
afternoon?'

'Because Mrs Sharp came and they
wanted us,' Cat said, puzzled.

'But we'd only been gone for an hour
or so, and we could have been just going
blackberrying. We hadn't even taken
our nightclothes,' Janet explained.
'Now do you see?'

Though Cat was indeed sure that
Janet had an obsession about withcraft,
and he was still feeling sulky and
unhelpful, he could not help seeing that
Janet had a point. 'A very nice witch,
then,' he conceded. 'I don't mind.'

'But, Cat, you do see how difficult
she's going to make it,' Janet said. 'Do
you? You know, you should be called
Mule, not Cat. If you don't want to
know a thing, you don't. How did you
get to be called Cat anyway?'

'That was just a joke Gwendolen
made,' said Cat. 'She always said I'd got
nine lives.'

'Gwendolen made jokes?' Janet asked
unbelievingly. She stopped, with an
arrested look, and turned stiffly away
from the mirror.

'Not usually,' said Cat.

'Great heavens! I wonder!' said Janet. 'In this place, where every other thing turns out to be enchanted, it almost must be! In which case, how horrible!' She pushed the mirror up until the glass faced the ceiling, jumped off the stool and raced to the wardrobe. She dragged Gwendolen's box out of it and sorted fiercely through it. 'Oh, I do hope I'm wrong! But I'm almost sure there were nine.'

'Nine what?' asked Cat.

Janet had found the bundle of letters addressed to Miss Caroline Chant. The red book of matches was tucked in front of it. Janet took the little book carefully out and chucked the letters back in the box. 'Nine matches,' she said, as she opened the book. 'And there are, too! Oh, good Lord, Cat! Five of them are burnt. Look.'

She held the book out to Cat. He saw there were indeed nine matches in it. The heads of the first two were black. The third was charred right down to the base. The fourth had a black head again. But the fifth had burnt so fiercely that

263

the paper behind was singed and there was a hole in the sandpaper beneath it. It was a wonder the whole book had not caught fire—or at least the last four matches. They were as new, however. Their heads were bright red, with yellowish oily paper below, and bright white cardboard below that.

'It does look like a charm of some kind,' Cat said.

'I know it is,' said Janet. 'These are your nine lives, Cat. How did you come to lose so many?'

Cat simply could not believe her. He was feeling surly and resistant anyway, and this was too much. 'They can't be,' he said. Even if he *had* nine lives, he knew he could only have lost three, and that was counting the time Gwendolen gave him cramps. The other two would be when he was born and on the paddleboat. But, as he thought this, Cat found he was remembering those four apparitions coming from the flaming bowl to join Gwendolen's gruesome procession. One had been a baby, one wet. The crippled one *had* seemed to have cramps. But why had there been four of them, when five matches were burnt?

Cat began shivering, and this made him all the more determined to prove Janet wrong.

'You couldn't have died in the night once or twice without noticing?' Janet wondered.

'Of course I didn't.' Cat reached down and took the book. 'Look, I'll prove it to you.' He tore the sixth match off and dragged it along the sandpaper.

Janet leapt up, shrieking him to stop. The match burst into flame.

So, almost at the same instant, did Cat himself.

CHAPTER FOURTEEN

Cat screamed. Flames burst out of him all over. He screamed again, and beat at himself with flaming hands, and went on screaming. They were pale, shimmering, transparent flames. They burst out through his clothes, and his shoes, his hair, across his face, so that, in

265

seconds, he was wrapped in pale flame from head to foot. He fell on the floor, still screaming, and rolled there, blazing.

Janet kept her presence of mind. She dragged up the nearest corner of the carpet and threw it over Cat. She had heard that this smothered flames. But it did not smother these. To Janet's horror, the pale ghostly flames came straight through the carpet as if it was not there, and played on the black underside of it more fiercely than ever. They did not burn the carpet, nor did they burn Janet's hands as she frantically rolled Cat over in the carpet, and then over again. But no matter how much carpet she wrapped round Cat, the flames still came through, and Cat went on blazing and screaming. His head was half outside the flaming bundle she had made of him, and it was a sheaf of flames. She could see his screaming face inside the fire.

Janet did the only other thing she could think of. She jumped up and screamed herself. 'Chrestomanci, Chrestomanci! Come *quickly*!'

The door burst open while she was still screaming. Janet had forgotten it was locked, but the lock did not bother Chrestomanci. She could see it sticking out from the edge of the door as he flung it open. She had forgotten there were guests to dinner too. She remembered when she saw Chrestomanci's lace ruffles, and his black velvet suit which glimmered all over like an opal, blue, crimson, yellow and green. But that did not seem to bother Chrestomanci either. He took one look at the flaming bundle on the floor and said 'Good God!' Then he was down on his elegant knees unwrapping the carpet as frantically as Janet had wrapped it.

'I'm awfully sorry. I thought that would help,' Janet stammered.

'It ought to have done,' said Chrestomanci, rolling Cat over, with flames whirling through, over and along his velvet arms. 'How did he do it?'

'He struck one of the matches. I told him—'

'You stupid child!' Chrestomanci was so angry that Janet burst into tears. He lugged at the last of the carpet and Cat rolled free, flaming like a straw faggot. He was not really screaming any more. He was making a long thin noise that had Janet covering her ears. Chrestomanci dived into the heart of the flames and found the book of matches. It was tightly clasped in Cat's right hand. 'Thank God he didn't have it in the left one,' he said. 'Go and turn your shower on. Quick!'

'Of course. Of course,' Janet sobbed, and raced to do it.

She fumbled with the taps and had just got a strong spray of cold water hissing into the sunken blue bath as Chrestomanci hurried in carrying Cat, in a ball of roaring flame. He dumped Cat down into the bath and held him there, turning him this way and that to get him wet all over.

Cat steamed and hissed. The water coming from the sprayhead shone like water against the sun, golden as the sun itself. It came down like a beam of light. And, as the bath began to fill up, Cat seemed to be turning and threshing in the pool of sunshine. He boiled it into golden bubbles. The room filled with steam. Coils of smoke drifted up from the bath, smelling thick and sweet. It was the same smell that Janet remembered from the morning she had first found herself there. As far as she could see through the smoke, Cat seemed to be turning black in the golden pool. But the water was wet. Chrestomanci was getting soaked.

'Don't you understand?' he said to Janet over his shoulder while he heaved at Cat to keep his head under the spray. 'You shouldn't go telling him things like this until the Castle has had time to work on him. He wasn't ready to understand. You've given him the most appalling shock.'

'I'm truly enormously sorry,' Janet said, crying heavily.

'We'll just have to make the best of it,' said Chrestomanci. 'I'll try and explain to him. Run along to the speaking tube at the end of the corridor and tell them to send me some brandy and a pot of strong tea.'

As Janet raced away, Cat found himself soaking wet, with water hissing down on him. He tried to roll away from it. Someone held him in it. A voice said insistently in his ear, 'Cat. Cat, will you listen to me. Do you understand? Cat, you've only got three lives left now.'

Cat knew that voice. 'You told me I'd got five when you spoke to me through Miss Larkins,' he grumbled.

'Yes, but you've only got three now. You'll have to be more careful,' said Chrestomanci.

Cat opened his eyes and looked up at him. Chrestomanci was fearfully wet. The usually smooth black hair was hanging over his forehead in wriggles, with drips on the ends. 'Oh. Was it you?' he said.

'Yes. You took a long time recognising me, didn't you?' said Chrestomanci. 'But then I didn't know you straight away when I saw you, either. I think you can come out of this water now.'

Cat was too weak to get out of the bath alone. But Chrestomanci heaved him out, stripped off his wet clothes, dried him and wrapped him in another towel in no time at all. Cat's legs kept folding. 'Up you come,' said Chrestomanci, and carried him again, to the blue velvet bed, and tucked him in it. 'Better now, Cat?'

Cat lay back, limp but luxurious, and nodded. 'Thanks. You've never called me Cat before.'

'Perhaps I should have done. You just might have understood.' Chrestomanci sat beside the bed, looking very serious. 'You do understand now?'

'The book of matches was my nine lives,' Cat said. 'And I've just burnt one. I know it was stupid, but I didn't believe it. How *can* I have nine lives?'

'You have three,' said Chrestomanci. 'Get that into your head. You did have nine. In some manner and by someone, they were put into that book of matches, and that book I am now going to put in my secret safe, sealed with the strongest enchantments I know. But that will only stop people using them. It won't stop you losing them yourself.'

Janet came hurrying in, still tearful, but very thankful to be of use. 'It's coming,' she said.

'Thank you,' said Chrestomanci, and he gave her a long, thoughtful look. Janet was sure he was going to accuse her of not being Gwendolen, but what he said was, 'You may as well hear this too, in order to prevent more accidents.'

'Can I get you a towel first?' Janet said humbly. 'You're so wet.'

'I'm drying out, thank you,' he said, smiling at her. 'Now listen. People with nine lives are very important and very rare. They only happen when, for one reason or another, there are no counterparts of them living in any other world. Then the lives that would have been spread out over a whole set of worlds get concentrated in one person. And so do all the talents that those other eight people might have had.'

Cat said, 'But I haven't any talents,' and Janet said at the same time, 'How rare *are* these people?'

'Extremely rare,' said Chrestomanci. 'Apart from Cat, the only other person with nine lives that I know of on this world is myself.'

'Really?' Cat was pleased and interested. 'Nine?'

'I did have nine. I've only got two now. I was even more careless than Cat,' Chrestomanci said. He sounded a little ashamed. 'Now I have to take care to keep each life separately in the safest place I can think of. I advise Cat to do the same.'

Janet's ready brain promptly got to work on this. 'Is one life here, and the other downstairs having supper at this moment?'

Chrestomanci laughed. 'It doesn't work like that. I—'

To Janet's disappointment, Euphemia hurried in with a tray and prevented Chrestomanci explaining how it did work. Mr Saunders came in on Euphemia's heels, still unable to find evening clothes that covered his wrists and ankles.

'Is he all right?' Euphemia asked anxiously. 'My Will was uttering threats, but if it was him I'll never speak to him again. And whatever happened to this carpet?'

Mr Saunders was looking at the wrinkled and heaped-up carpet too. 'What did it?' he said. 'There were surely enough charms in this carpet to stop any kind of accident.'

'I know,' said Chrestomanci. 'But this

273

was amazingly strong.' The two of them looked at one another significantly.

Then everyone fussed over Cat. He had a most enjoyable time. Mr Saunders sat him up on pillows, and Euphemia put him in a nightshirt and then stroked Cat's head, just as if he had never confessed to turning her into a frog. 'It wasn't Will,' Cat said to her. 'It was me.' Chrestomanci gave him a fierce swig of brandy and then made him drink a cup of sweet tea. Janet had a cup of tea too, and felt much better for it. Mr Saunders helped Euphemia straighten the carpet, and then asked if he should strengthen the charms in it.

'Dragon's blood might do the trick,' he suggested.

'Frankly, I don't think anything will,' said Chrestomanci. 'Leave it.' He got up and turned the mirror straight. 'Do you mind sleeping tonight in Cat's room?' he asked Janet. 'I want to be able to keep an eye on Cat.'

Janet looked from the mirror to Chrestomanci, and her face became very pink. 'Er,' she said. 'I've been making faces—'

Chrestomanci laughed. Mr Saunders was so amused that he had to sit on the blue velvet stool. 'I suppose it serves me right,' said Chrestomanci. 'Some of the faces were highly original.'

Janet laughed too, a little foolishly.

Cat lay, feeling comfortable and almost cheerful. For a while, everyone was there, settling him in. Then there seemed only to be Janet, talking as usual.

'I'm so glad you're all right,' she said. 'Why did I open my big mouth about those matches? I had the dreaded umjams when you suddenly flared up, and when the carpet didn't work, the only thing I could think of was to yell for Chrestomanci. I *was* right. He came before the words were out of my mouth, even though the door was locked. It was still locked when he opened it, but the lock isn't broken, because I tried it. So he *is* an enchanter. And he ruined a suit over you, Cat, and didn't seem to mind, so I think that when he isn't being like freezing fog over the Grampians, he's really very nice. This isn't for the benefit of the mirror. I mean it. I suppose that

275

mirror is the magic equivalent of . . .'

Cat thought he had been meaning to say something about freezing fog in the Grampians, but he drifted away to sleep while Janet talked, feeling snug and cared-for.

★   ★   ★

He woke on Sunday morning, quite the opposite: cold and quivering. This afternoon, he was due to be turned into a frog or face a tiger—and a rather heavy strong tiger Will Suggins would make too, he thought. Beyond the tiger—if there was a beyond—lay the horrors of Monday without magic. Julia and Roger might help there, except that it would be no use when Mr Baslam came on Wednesday and demanded twenty pounds Cat knew he could not get. Mr Nostrum was no help. Mrs Sharp was even less. The only hope seemed to be to take Janet and some dragon's blood to the forbidden garden and try to get away.

Cat climbed out of bed to go and get some dragon's blood from Mr

Saunders's workshop. Euphemia came in with his breakfast on a tray, and he had to climb back into bed again. Euphemia was quite as kind as she had been last night. Cat felt bad. And when he had finished breakfast, Milly came. She scooped Cat off his pillows and hugged him.

'You poor silly darling! Thank goodness you're all right. I was aching to come and see you last night, but someone had to stay with our poor guests. Now, you're to stay in bed all today, and you must ask for anything you want. What would you like?'

'I couldn't have some dragon's blood, could I?' Cat asked hopefully.

Milly laughed. 'Good heavens, Eric! You go and have that fearsome accident and then you ask for the most dangerous stuff in the world. No, you may not have dragon's blood. It's one of the few things in the Castle that really are forbidden.'

'Like Chrestomanci's garden?' Cat asked.

'*Not* quite like that,' Milly answered. 'The garden is old as the hills and stuffed with magic of every kind. That's dangerous in another way. Everything's stronger there. You'll be taken into the garden when you know enough magic to understand it. But dragon's blood is so harmful that I'm never happy even when Michael uses it. You're on no account to touch any.'

Julia and Roger came in next, dressed ready for church, with armfuls of books and toys and a great many interested questions. They were so kind that Cat was quite unhappy by the time Janet arrived. He did not want to leave the Castle. He felt he was truly settling in to it.

'That lump of dough is still stuck to your carpet,' Janet said gloomily, which made Cat feel rather less settled. 'I've just been seeing Chrestomanci, and it *is* hard to be punished for other people's sins,' Janet went on, 'even though I've been rewarded with the sight of a sky-blue dressing-gown with golden lions on it.'

'I've not seen that one,' said Cat.

'I think he has one for every day of the week,' said Janet. 'All he needed was a flaming sword. He forbade me to go to church. The vicar won't have me because of what Gwendolen did last Sunday. And I was so cross at being blamed for it that I'd got my mouth open to say I wasn't Gwendolen, when I remembered that if I went to church I'd have to wear that stupid white hat with little holes in it—can he *hear* through that mirror, do you think?'

'No,' said Cat. 'Just see. Or he'd know all about you. I'm glad you're staying behind. We can go and get the dragon's blood while they're at church.'

Janet kept watch at the window to see when the Family left. After about half an hour, she said, 'Here they are at last, walking in a crowd down the avenue. All the men have got toppers, but Chrestomanci looks as if he's come out of a shop window. Who *are* they all, Cat? Who's the old lady in purple mittens, and the young one in green, and the little fellow who's always talking?'

'I've no idea,' said Cat. He scrambled out of bed and scuttled up to his room to find some clothes. He felt perfectly well—marvellously well, in fact. He danced round his room while he put on his shirt. He sang putting on his trousers. Even the cold lump of dough on the carpet could not damp his spirits. He whistled tying his boots.

Janet came into the room as Cat was shooting out of it, pulling on his jacket and beaming with health. 'I don't know,' Janet said, as Cat shot past her and hammered away down the stairs. 'Dying must agree with you, or something.'

'Hurry up!' Cat called from the bottom of the stairs. 'It's on the other side of the Castle from here. Milly says dragon's blood is very dangerous, so don't you touch it. I can spare a life on it and you can't.'

Janet wanted to remark that Cat had not spared the last one very easily, but she never caught Cat up sufficiently. Cat whirled through the green corridors and stormed up the winding stairs to Mr Saunders's room, and Janet only reached him when he was actually inside it. Then there was too much else to take up her attention.

The room was heavy with the scent of stale magic. Though it was much the same as when Cat had seen it before, Mr Saunders had tidied it a little for Sunday. The cresset was out. The torts and limbecks and other vessels were all clean. The books and scrolls had been piled in heaps on the second bench. The five-pointed star was still there, blazoned on the floor, but there was a new set of signs chalked on the third bench, and the mummified animal had been neatly laid at one end of it.

Janet was immensely interested. 'It's like a laboratory,' she said, 'except that it isn't. What weird things! Oh, I see the dragon's blood. Does he need all that huge jar? He won't miss a bit out of that lot.'

There was a rustling at the end of the third bench. Janet's head jerked towards it. The mummified creature was twitching and spreading its filmy little wings.

'It did that before,' said Cat. 'I think it's all right.'

He was not so sure, however, when the creature stretched and got to its dog-like feet, yawning. The yawn showed them dozens of small sharp teeth and also let out a cloud of bluish smoke. The creature ran pattering along the bench towards them. The little wings rattled on its back as it came, and two small puffs of smoke streamed behind it from its nostrils. It stopped at the edge of the bench to look up at them inquisitively from a melting glitter of golden eyes. They backed nervously away from it.

'It's alive!' said Janet. 'I think it's a small dragon.'

'Of course I am,' said the dragon, which made both of them jump violently. Even more alarming, tiny flames played out of its mouth as it spoke, and they could feel the heat from them where they stood.

'I didn't know you could talk,' said Cat.

'I speak English quite well,' said the dragon, flickering flame. 'Why do you want my blood?'

They looked guiltily at the great jar of powder on the shelf. 'Is that all yours?' said Cat.

'If Mr Saunders is making it give blood all the time, I think that's rather cruel,' Janet said.

'Oh, that!' said the dragon. 'That's powdered blood from older dragons. They sell it to people. You can't have any of that.'

'Why not?' said Cat.

'Because I don't want you to,' said the dragon, and a regular roll of fire came from its mouth, making them back away again. 'How would you like to see me taking human blood and playing games with it?'

Though Cat felt the dragon had a point here, Janet did not. 'It doesn't worry me,' she said. 'Where I come from we have blood transfusions and blood-banks. Dad once showed me some of my blood under a microscope.'

'It worries *me*,' said the dragon, uttering another roll of fire. 'My mother was killed by unlawful blood-stealers.' It crept to the very end of the bench and stared up at Janet. The flickers in its golden eyes melted and changed and melted again. It was like being looked at by two small golden kaleidoscopes. 'I was too small to hold enough blood,' it flickered softly to Janet, 'so they left me. I'd have died if Chrestomanci hadn't found me. So you see why it worries me?'

'Yes,' said Janet. 'What do baby dragons feed on? Milk?'

'Michael tried me with milk, but I didn't like it,' said the dragon. 'I have minced steak now, and I'm growing beautifully. When I'm big enough, he's going to take me back, but meanwhile I'm helping him with his magic. I'm a great help.'

'Are you?' said Janet. 'What do you do?'

'I find old things he can't find himself.' The dragon fell into a flickering croon. 'I fetch him animals from the abyss—old golden creatures, things with wings, pearl-eyed monsters from the deep sea, and whispering plants from long ago.' It stopped and looked at Janet with its head on one side. 'That was easy,' it remarked to Cat. 'I've always wanted to do that, but no one let me before.' It sighed a long blue fume of smoke. 'I wish I was bigger. I could eat her now.'

Cat took an alarmed look at Janet and found her staring like a sleep-walker, with a silly smile on her face. 'Of all the mean tricks!' he said.

'I think I'll just have a nibble,' said the dragon.

Cat realised it was being playful. 'I'll wring your neck if you do,' he said. 'Haven't you got anything else to play with?'

'You sound just like Michael,' said the dragon in a sulky roll of smoke. 'I'm bored with mice.'

'Tell him to take you for walks.' Cat took Janet's arm and shook her. Janet came to herself with a little jump and seemed quite unaware that anything had happened to her. 'And I can't help the way you feel,' said Cat to the dragon. 'I need some dragon's blood.' He pulled Janet well out of range, just to be on the safe side, and picked up a little china crucible from the next bench.

The dragon hunched up irritably and scratched itself like a dog under the chin until its wings rattled. 'Michael says dragon's blood always does harm somewhere,' it said, 'even when an adept uses it. If you're not careful, it costs a life.'

285

Cat and Janet looked at one another through the smoke it had made with its speech. 'Well, I can spare one,' said Cat. He took the glass stopper off the big jar and scooped up some brown powder in the crucible. It had a strong, strange smell.

'I suppose Chrestomanci manages all right with two lives,' Janet said nervously.

'But he's rather special,' said the dragon. It was standing on the very edge of the bench, rattling with anxiety. Its golden eyes followed Cat's hands as he wrapped the crucible in his handkerchief and pushed the bundle cautiously into his pocket. It seemed so worried that Cat went over to it and, a little nervously, rubbed it under the chin where it had been scratching. The dragon stretched its neck and pressed against his fingers. The smoke came out of its nostrils in purring puffs.

'Don't worry,' Cat said. 'I've got three lives left, you see.'

'That explains why I like you,' said the dragon, and almost fell off the bench in its effort to follow Cat's fingers.

'Don't go yet!'

'We've got to.' Cat pushed the dragon back on the bench and patted its head. Once he was used to it, he found he did not mind touching its warm horny hide a bit. 'Goodbye.'

'Goodbye,' said the dragon.

They left it staring after them like a dog whose master has gone for a walk without it.

'I think it's bored,' Cat said when he had shut the door.

'It's a shame! It's only a baby,' said Janet. She stopped on the first turn of the stair. 'Let's go back and take it for a walk. It was sweet!'

Cat was sure that if Janet did any such thing, she would come to herself to find the dragon browsing on her legs. 'It wasn't that sweet,' he said. 'And we'll have to go to the garden straight away now. It's going to tell Mr Saunders we took some dragon's blood as soon as it sees him.'

'Yes, I suppose it does make a difference that it can talk,' Janet agreed. 'We'd better hurry then.'

Cat walked very carefully through the

Castle, down and out of doors, and kept
a hand on his pocket in case of accidents.
He was afraid he might arrive at the
forbidden garden with one life less. He
seemed to have lost three of his lives so
easily. That kept puzzling him. From
the look of those matches, losing life
number five ought to have been as much
of a disaster as losing the sixth one last
night. But he had not noticed it go at all.
He could not understand it. His lives did
not seem to be properly attached to him,
like ordinary people's. But at least he
knew there were no other Cat Chants to
be dragged into trouble in this world,
when he left it.

CHAPTER FIFTEEN

It was a glorious start-of-autumn day,
with everything green and gold, hot and
still. There was not a soul around, and
very little sound except the lonely
crunch of Cat's and Janet's feet as they
hurried through the formal garden.
Halfway through the orchard, Janet

said, 'If the garden we want looks like a ruined castle, we're going away from it now.'

Cat could have sworn that they were heading straight for it, but, sure enough, when he stopped and looked round, the high sun-soaked old wall was right behind them. And now he came to think of it, he could not remember how he and Gwendolen had got to it before.

They turned back and walked towards the high wall. All they found was the long, low wall of the orchard. There was no gate in it, and the forbidden garden was beyond it. They went along the orchard wall to the nearest gate. Whereupon they were in the rose garden, and the ruined wall was behind them again, towering above the orchard.

'This couldn't be an enchantment to stop people getting into it, could it?' said Janet, as they plodded through the orchard again.

'I think it must be,' said Cat. And they were in the formal garden again, with the high wall behind them.

'They'll be coming out of church before we've found it at this rate,' Janet said anxiously.

'Try keeping it in the corner of your eye and not going straight to it,' said Cat.

They did that. They walked slantwise with the garden, not really looking at it. It seemed to keep pace with them. And suddenly, they came out somehow beyond the orchard into a steep, walled path. Up at the top of it stood the high old wall, with its stairway masked by hollyhocks and bright with snapdragons, breathing warmth out of its crumbling stones into their worried faces. Neither of them dared look straight at the tall ruins, even while they were running up the path. But the wall was still there, when they reached the end, and so was the overgrown stair.

The stair made a nerve-racking climb. They had to go up it twice as high as a house, with one side of themselves pressed against the hot stones of the wall, and a sheer drop on the other side. The stairs were frighteningly old and irregular. And they grew hotter and hotter. Towards the end, Cat had to keep his head tipped up to the trees hanging over the top of the ruins, because looking anywhere else began to make him dizzy. He had glimpses of the Castle in the distance from more angles than he would have thought possible. He suspected that the ruins he was on were moving about.

There was a notch in the wall at the top, not like a proper entrance at all. They swung themselves in through it, secret and guilty, and found the ground beyond worn smooth, as if other people had been coming that way for centuries. There were trees, thick and dark and close together. It was wonderfully cool. The smoothly worn path twined among them. Janet and Cat stole along it. As they went, the trees, as closely-growing trees often seem to do when you walk among them, appeared to move this way and that and spread into different distances. But Cat was not altogether sure it was only an appearance.

One new distance opened into a dell. And then they were in the dell.

'What a lovely place!' Janet whispered. 'But how peculiar!'

The little dip was full of spring flowers. Daffodils, scillas, snowdrops, hyacinths and tiny tulips were all growing there in September in the most improbable profusion. There was a slight chill in the dip, which may have accounted for it. Janet and Cat picked their way among these flowers, shivering a little. There were the scents of spring, chilly and heady, clean and wild, but strong with magic. Before they had taken two steps, Cat and Janet were smiling gently. Another step and they were laughing.

'Oh look!' said Janet. 'There's a cat.'

It was a large stripy tom. It stood arched suspiciously beside a clump of primroses, not sure whether to run away or not. It looked at Janet. It looked at Cat. And Cat knew it. Though it was firmly and definitely a cat, there was just a suggestion of a violin about the shape of its face.

He laughed. Everything made him happy in that place. 'That's old Fiddle,' he said. 'He used to be my violin. What's he doing here?'

Janet knelt down and held out her hand. 'Here, Fiddle. Here, puss.' Fiddle's nature must have been softened by being in that dell. He let Janet rub his chin and stroke him. Then in the most unheard-of way, he let Janet pick him up and stand up hugging him. He even purred. Janet's face glowed. She could almost have been Gwendolen coming home from a witchcraft lesson, except that she looked kinder. She winked at Cat. 'I love all kinds of Cat!'

Cat laughed. He put out his left hand and stroked Fiddle's head. It felt strange. He could feel the wood of the violin. He took his hand away quickly.

They went on through a white spread of narcissi, smelling like paradise, Janet still carrying Fiddle. There had been no white flowers until then. Cat began to be almost sure that the garden was moving round them of its own accord. When he stepped among bluebells, and then big red tulips, he was sure. He almost—but not quite—saw the trees softly and gently sliding about at the sides of what he could see. They slid him among buttercups and cow-parsley, into a sunny, sloping stretch. And here was a wild rose, tangled with a creeper covered in great blue flowers. Cat could definitely feel the sliding movement now. They were being moved round and down somehow. If he thought about the way the garden had also been moving about in the Castle grounds, he started to feel almost as sick as he did in the car. He found it was best just to keep walking and looking.

When they slid through the trees among flowers of high summer, Janet noticed too. 'Aren't we getting a lightning tour of the year?' she said. 'I feel as if I'm running down a moving staircase.'

It was more than the ordinary year. Fig-trees, olives and date-palms moved them round into a small desert, where there were cacti like tormented cucumbers and spiny green armchairs. Some had bright flowers on them. The sun burnt down. But they had hardly time to get uncomfortable before the trees circled around them again and brought them into a richer, sadder light, and autumn flowers. They had barely got used to that, when the trees put out berries, turned amber and lost their leaves. They moved towards a thick

294

holly, full of red berries. It was colder. Fiddle did not like this part. He struggled out of Janet's arms and ran away to warmer climes.

'Which are the gates to other worlds?' Janet said, brought back to a sense of purpose.

'Soon, I think,' said Cat. He felt them coming to the centre of the garden. He had seldom felt anything magical so strongly.

The trees and bushes round them now were embalmed in frost. They could see bright berries in bright casings of ice. Yet Janet had scarcely time to rub her arms and shiver, before a tree met them that was a wintry mass of pink blossom. Straight stalks of winter jasmine hung from the next, in lines of small yellow stars. And then came a mighty black thorn tree, twisted in all directions. It was just putting out a few white blossoms.

As it took them in under its dark hood, Janet looked up into its black twistings. 'The one at Glastonbury looks like this,' she said. 'They say it blooms at Christmas.'

Then Cat knew they were in the heart of the garden. They were in a small bowl of meadowland. All the trees were up round the edges, except one. And here it seemed the right season of the year, because the apples were just ripening on that one tree. It stood leaning over the centre of the meadow, not quite over-shadowing the queer ruin there. As Janet and Cat passed quietly towards this place, they found a little spring of water near the roots of the apple tree, which bubbled up from nowhere, and bubbled away again into the earth almost at once. Janet thought the clear water looked unusually golden. It reminded her of the water from the shower when it stopped Cat burning.

The ruins were two sides of a broken archway. There was a slab of stone which must have fallen from the top of the arch lying nearby at the foot of the tree. There was no other sign of a gate.

'I think this is it,' said Cat. He felt very sad to be leaving.

'I think it is, too,' Janet agreed in an awed, muffled voice. 'I feel a bit miserable to be going, as a matter of fact.

296

How *do* we go?'

'I'm going to try sprinkling a pinch of dragon's blood in the archway,' said Cat.

He fumbled out the crucible wrapped in his handkerchief from his pocket. He smelt the strong smell of the dragon's blood and knew he was doing wrong. It was wrong to bring this harmful stuff into a place that was so strongly magic in such a different way.

But, since he did not know what else to do, Cat carefully took a pinch of the smelly brown powder between the finger and thumb of his right hand, wrapped the crucible away again with his left hand, and then, carefully and guiltily, sprinkled the powder between the pillars of broken stone.

The air between the pillars quivered like air that is hot. The piece of sunny meadow they could see beyond grew misty, then milky pale, then dark. The darkness cleared slowly, away into the corners of the space, and they found they could see into a huge room. There seemed acres of it. All of it was covered in a carpet of a rather ugly playing-card sort of design in red, blue and yellow.

The room was full of people. They reminded Cat of playing-cards too, because they were dressed in stiff bulky clothes in flat bright colours. They were all trailing about, this way and that, looking important and agitated. The air between them and the garden was still quivering and, somehow, Cat knew they would not be able to get into the huge room.

'This is not right,' said Janet. 'Where is it?'

Cat was just about to say that he did not know either, when he saw Gwendolen. She was being carried by, quite near, on a sort of bed with handholds. The eight men carrying it all wore bulky golden uniforms. The bed was gold, with gold hangings and gold cushions. Gwendolen was dressed in even bulkier clothes than the rest, that were white and gold, and her hair was done up into a high golden headdress which may have been a crown. From the way she was behaving, she was certainly a queen. She nodded to some of the important people and they leapt eagerly to the side of her bed and listened with feverish intelligence to what she was saying. She waved to some others, and they ran to do things. She made a sign at another person and he fell on his knees, begging for mercy. He was still begging when other people dragged him away. Gwendolen smiled as if this amused her. By this time, the golden bed was right beside the archway, and the space was a turmoil of people racing to do what Gwendolen wanted.

And Gwendolen saw Cat and Janet. Cat knew she did, from the expression of surprise and faint annoyance on her face. Maybe she worked some magic of her own, or maybe the magic in the dragon's blood was simply used up. Whatever it was, the broken archway turned dark again, then milky, then to mist; and finally, there was nothing but meadow again between the pillars, and the air had stopped shimmering.

'That was Gwendolen,' Cat said.

'I thought it was,' Janet said unappreciatively. 'She'll get fat if she has herself carried about like that all the time.'

'She was enjoying herself,' Cat said

wistfully.

'I could see that,' said Janet. 'But how do we find my world?'

Cat was not at all sure. 'Shall we try going round to the other side of the arch?'

'Seems reasonable,' Janet agreed. She started to walk round the pillars, and stopped. 'We'd better get it right this time, Cat. You can only afford one more try. Or didn't you lose a life on that one?'

'I didn't feel—' Cat began.

Then Mr Nostrum was suddenly standing in the broken arch. He was holding the postcard Cat had sent to Mrs Sharp, and he was cross and flustered.

'My dear boy,' he said to Cat, 'I told you two-thirty, not midday. It was the merest chance that I had my hand on your signature. Let us hope all is not lost.' He turned and called over his shoulder, apparently into the empty meadow, 'Come on, William. The wretched boy seems to have misunderstood me, but the spell is clearly working. Don't forget to bring the—ah—equipment with you.'

He stepped out from between the

pillars, and Cat backed away before him. Everything seemed to have gone very quiet. The leaves of the apple tree did not stir, and the small bubbling from the little spring changed to a soft, slow dripping. Cat had a strong suspicion that he and Janet had done something terrible. Janet was beyond the archway with her hands to her mouth, looking horrified. She was suddenly hidden by the large figure of Mr William Nostrum, who popped into being from nowhere between the two pillars. He had a coil of rope round one arm, and there were shiny things sticking out of the pockets of his frock-coat. His eyes were swivelling in an agitated way. He was a little out of breath.

'Premature but successful, Henry,' he puffed. 'The rest have been summoned.'

William Nostrum stepped imposingly out beneath the apple tree beside his brother. The ground shook a little. The garden was quite silent. Cat backed away again and found that the little spring had stopped flowing. There was nothing but a muddy hole left. Cat was quite certain now that he and Janet had done something terrible.

Behind the Nostrums, other people came hurrying through the broken archway. The first one who came was one of the Accredited Witches from further down Coven Street, puce in the face and very startled. She had been to church in her Sunday best: a monster of a hat with fruit and flowers in it, and a black and red satin dress. Most of the people who followed her were in Sunday best too: warlocks in blue serge and hard hats, witches in silk and bombazine and hats of all shapes and sizes, respectable-looking necromancers in frock-coats like William Nostrum's, skinny sorcerers in black, and quite a sprinkling of impressive wizards, who had either been to church in long black cloaks, or playing golf in very freckled plus-fours. They came crowding between the pillars, first by twos and threes and then by sixes and sevens, all a little hasty and startled. Among them Cat recognised most of the witches and fortune-tellers from Coven Street, though he did not see either Mrs Sharp or Miss Larkins— but this may have been simply that, in no time at all, he was being jostled this way and that in the middle of a large and steadily growing crowd.

William Nostrum was shouting to each group who hurried through, 'Spread out. Spread out up the meadow. Surround the gate there! Leave no avenue of escape.'

Janet forced her way among them and seized Cat's arm. 'Cat! What have we done? Don't tell me these aren't all witches and warlocks, because I won't believe you!'

'Ah, my dear Gwendolen!' said Mr Henry Nostrum. 'Plan Two is under way.'

By this time, the sloping sides of the meadow were crowded with witches and warlocks. The ground quivered to their trampling and buzzed with their cheerful conversation. There were hundreds of them—a nodding of garish hats and shiny toppers, like the audience at the opening of a bazaar.

As soon as the last necromancer had hurried between the pillars, Henry Nostrum put a heavy possessive hand on Cat's shoulder. Cat wondered uneasily whether it was just an accident that it was the same hand which held his postcard to Mrs Sharp. He saw that the Willing Warlock had stationed himself by one of the broken pillars, blue-chinned and cheerful as ever in his tight Sunday suit. Mr William Nostrum had put as much of himself as would go behind the other pillar, and, for some reason, he had taken off his heavy silver watch-chain and was swinging it in one hand.

'Now, my dear Gwendolen,' said Henry Nostrum, 'would you care for the honour of summoning Chrestomanci?'

'I—I'd rather not,' said Janet.

'Then I'll take it upon myself,' said Henry Nostrum, perfectly well pleased. He cleared his throat and shouted in a fluting tenor, 'Chrestomanci! Chrestomanci! Come to me.'

And Chrestomanci was standing between the pillars.

Chrestomanci must have been on his way up the avenue from church. He had his tall grey hat in one hand, and, with the other, he was in the act of putting his prayer-book into the pocket of his

304

beautiful dove grey coat. The assembled witches and necromancers greeted him with a sort of groaning sigh. Chrestomanci blinked round at them, in his mildest and most bewildered way. He became even vaguer and more bewildered when he happened to see Cat and Janet.

Cat opened his mouth to shout at Chrestomanci to go away. But the Willing Warlock leapt on Chrestomanci the moment he appeared. He was growling. His finger-nails were growing into claws and his teeth into fangs.

Chrestomanci stuffed the prayer-book into his pocket and turned his vague look on the Willing Warlock. The Willing Warlock stood still in mid-air and shrank. He shrank so fast, he made a whirring sound. Then he was a small brown caterpillar. He dropped to the grass and wriggled there. But, while he was still shrinking, William Nostrum pounced out from behind the other pillar and deftly wrapped his watch-chain round Chrestomanci's right hand.

'*Behind you!*' shrieked Cat and Janet, too late.

After barely one wriggle, the caterpillar burst up out of the grass and became the Willing Warlock again, a little dishevelled, but very pleased with himself. He threw himself on Chrestomanci again. As for Chrestomanci, it was plain that the watch-chain had somehow disabled him completely. There was a second or so of furious struggle in the archway, while the Willing Warlock tried to grab Chrestomanci in both brawny arms, and Chrestomanci tried to get the watch-chain off his wrist using his left hand, and William Nostrum hung on to it fiercely. None of them used any magic, and Chrestomanci seemed only able to shoulder the Willing Warlock weakly aside. After two attempts, the Willing Warlock wrapped his arms round Chrestomanci from behind and William Nostrum dragged a pair of silver handcuffs from his pocket and snapped them on both Chrestomanci's wrists.

There was a scream of triumph from under the nodding hats of the audience—the scream of true witchcraft, which made the sunlight tremble. Chrestomanci, even more dishevelled than the Willing Warlock, was dragged out from between the pillars. His tall grey hat rolled near Cat's feet and Henry Nostrum stamped on it, with the greatest satisfaction. Cat tried to get out from under Henry Nostrum's hand while he did it. And he found he could not move. Mr Nostrum had seen to that with Mrs Sharp's postcard. Cat had to face the fact that he was as helpless as Chrestomanci seemed to be.

'So it is true!' Henry Nostrum said joyously, as the Willing Warlock bundled Chrestomanci towards the apple tree. 'The touch of silver conquers Chrestomanci—the great Chrestomanci!'

'Yes. Isn't it a nuisance?' Chrestomanci remarked. He was dragged to the apple tree and pushed against it. William Nostrum hurried over to his brother and pulled the watch-chain off Henry's bulging waistcoat. Two silver watch-chains from two such ample brothers were more than enough to tie Chrestomanci to the tree. William Nostrum hastily twisted the ends into

307

two charmed knots and stood back rubbing his hands. The audience screamed eldritch laughter and clapped. Chrestomanci sagged as if he were tired. His hair hung over his face, his tie was under his left ear, and there was green from the bark of the tree all over his dove grey coat. Cat felt somehow ashamed to look at him in that state. But Chrestomanci seemed quite composed. 'Now you've got me all tied up in silver, what do you propose doing?' he said.

William Nostrum's eyes swirled joyfully about. 'Oh, the worst we can, my dear sir,' he said. 'Be assured of that. We're sick of you imposing restraints on us, you see. Why shouldn't we go out and conquer other worlds? Why shouldn't we use dragon's blood? Why shouldn't we be as wicked as we want? Answer me that, sir!'

'You might find the answer for yourself, if you thought,' Chrestomanci suggested. But his voice was drowned in the yelling from the assembled witches and necromancers. While they shouted, Janet began edging quietly towards the tree. She supposed Cat dared not move

308

with Henry Nostrum's hand on his shoulder, and she felt someone ought to do something.

'Oh, yes,' said Henry Nostrum, cock-a-hoop with pleasure. 'We are taking the arts of magic into our own hands today. This world will be ours by this evening. Come Hallowe'en, dear sir, we shall be going out to conquer every other world we know. We are going to destroy you, my dear fellow, and your power. But before we do that, of course, we shall have to destroy this garden.'

Chrestomanci looked thoughtfully down at his hands, hanging limply in the silver handcuffs. 'I shouldn't advise that,' he said. 'This garden has things in it from the dawn of all the worlds. It's a good deal stronger than I am. You'd be striking at the roots of witchcraft—and you'd find it shockingly hard to destroy.'

'Ah,' said Henry Nostrum. 'But we know we can't destroy you unless we destroy the garden, my wily sir. And don't think we don't know how to destroy the garden.' He lifted his free hand and clapped Cat on the other

309

shoulder with it. 'The means are here.'

Janet, at that moment, stumbled over the block of stone that lay in the grass near the apple tree. 'Dratitude!' she said and fell heavily across it. The audience pointed and screamed with laughter, which annoyed her very much. She glared round the circle of Sunday bonnets and hats.

'Up you get, dear Gwendolen,' Henry Nostrum said gleefully. 'It's young Cat who has to go on there.' He put an arm round the helpless Cat, plucked him off the ground and carried him towards the block of stone. William Nostrum, bustled up beaming and uncoiling his rope. The Willing Warlock bounced up willingly to help too.

Cat was so terrified that he managed somehow to break the spell. He twisted out of Henry Nostrum's arms and ran for all he was worth towards the two pillars, trying to fetch out his dragon's blood as he ran. It was only a few steps to run. But naturally every witch, warlock, necromancer and wizard there instantly cast a spell. The thick smell of magic coiled round the meadow. Cat's legs felt like two lead posts. His heart hammered. He felt himself running in slow-motion, slower and slower, like a clockwork toy running down. He heard Janet scream at him to run, but he could not move any longer. He stuck just in front of the ruined archway, and he was stiff as a board. It was all he could do to breathe.

The Nostrum brothers and the Willing Warlock collected him from there, and wound the rope round his stiff body. Janet did her best to prevent them.

'Oh please stop! What are you doing?'

'Now, now, Gwendolen,' Henry Nostrum said, rather perplexed. 'You know perfectly well. I explained to you most carefully that the garden has to be disenchanted by cutting the throat of an innocent child on that slab of stone there. You agreed it must be so.'

'I didn't! It wasn't me!' said Janet.

'Be quiet!' Chrestomanci said, from the tree. 'Do you want to be put in Cat's place?'

Janet stared at him, and went on staring as all the implications struck her.

311

While she stared, Cat, stiff as a mummy and wound in rope, was carried by the Willing Warlock and dumped rather painfully down on the block of stone. Cat stared resentfully at the Willing Warlock. He had always seemed so friendly. Apart from that, Cat was not as frightened as he might have been. Of course Gwendolen had known he had lives to spare. But he hoped his throat would heal after they cut it. He was bound to be very uncomfortable until it did. He turned his eyes up to Janet, meaning to give her a reassuring look.

To his astonishment, Janet was snatched away backwards into nothingness. The only thing which remained of her was a yell of surprise. And the same yell rumbled round the meadow. Everyone there was quite as astonished as Cat.

'Oh, good!' Gwendolen said, from the other side of the stone. 'I got here in time.'

Everyone stared at her. Gwendolen came from between the pillars, dusting off the dragon's blood from her fingers with one of Cat's school essays. Cat

312

could see his signature at the top: *Eric Emelius Chant, 26 Coven St., Wolvercote, England, Europe, The World, The Universe*—it was his all right. Gwendolen still had her hair up in that strange headdress, but she had taken off the massive golden robes. She had on what must have amounted to underclothes in her new world. They were more magnificent than any of Chrestomanci's dressing-gowns.

'Gwendolen!' exclaimed Henry Nostrum. He pointed to the space Janet had vanished from. 'What—who—?'

'Just a replacement,' Gwendolen explained, in her airiest way. 'I saw her and Cat here just now, so I knew—' She noticed Chrestomanci limply tied to the apple tree. 'Oh good! You caught him! Just a moment.' She marched over to Chrestomanci and held up her golden underclothes in order to kick him hard on both shins. 'Take that! And that!' Chrestomanci did not try to pretend the kicks did not hurt. He doubled up. The toes of Gwendolen's shoes were as pointed as nails.

'Now, where was I?' Gwendolen said,

turning back to the Nostrum brothers. 'Oh, yes. I thought I'd better come back because I wanted to see the fun, and I remembered I'd forgotten to tell you Cat has nine lives. You'll have to kill him several times, I'm afraid.'

'*Nine lives!*' shouted Henry Nostrum. 'You foolish girl!'

After that, there was such a shouting and outcry from every witch and warlock in the meadow, that no one could have heard anything else. From where Cat lay, he could see William Nostrum leaning towards Gwendolen, red in the face, both eyes whirling, bawling furiously at her, and Gwendolen leaning forward to shout back. As the noise died down a little, he heard William Nostrum booming, 'Nine lives! If he has nine lives, you stupid girl, *that means he's an enchanter in his own right!*'

'I'm not stupid!' Gwendolen yelled back. 'I know that as well as you do! I've been using his magic ever since he was a baby. But I couldn't go on using it if you were going to kill him, could I? That's why I had to go away. I think it was nice of me to come back and tell you. So there!'

'How *can* you have used his magic?' demanded Henry Nostrum, even more put out than his brother.

'I just did,' said Gwendolen. 'He never minds.'

'I *do* mind, rather,' Cat said from his uncomfortable slab. 'I *am* here, you know.'

Gwendolen looked down at him as if she was rather surprised that he was. But before she could say anything to Cat, William Nostrum was loudly shushing for silence. He was very agitated. He took a long shiny thing out of his pocket and nervously bent it about.

'Silence!' he said. 'We've gone too far to draw back now. We'll just have to discover the boy's weak point. We certainly can't kill him unless we find it. He must have one. All enchanters do.' So saying, William Nostrum rounded on Cat and pointed the shiny thing at him. Cat was appalled to see that it was a long silver knife. The knife pointed at his face, even though William Nostrum's eyes did not. 'What is your weak point, boy? Out with it.'

Cat was not saying. It seemed the only chance he had of keeping any of his lives.

'I know,' said Gwendolen. 'I did it. I put all his lives into a book of matches. They were easier to use like that. It's in my room in the Castle. Shall I get it?'

Everyone Cat could see from his uncomfortable position looked relieved to hear this. 'That's all right then,' said Henry Nostrum. 'Can he be killed without burning a match?'

'Oh yes,' said Gwendolen. 'He drowned once.'

'So the question,' said William Nostrum, very much relieved, 'is simply how many lives he has left. How many have you, boy?' The knife pointed at Cat again.

Again Cat was not saying.

'He doesn't know,' Gwendolen said impatiently. 'I had to use quite a few. He lost one being born and another being drowned. And I used one to put him in the book of matches. It gave him cramps, for some reason. Then that toad tied up in silver there wouldn't give me magic lessons and took my witchcraft away, so I had to fetch another of Cat's

316

lives in the night and make it send me to my nice new world. He was awfully disobliging about it, but he did it. And that was the end of that life. Oh, I nearly forgot! I put his fourth life into that violin he kept playing, to turn it into a cat—Fiddle—remember, Mr Nostrum?'

Henry Nostrum clutched his two wings of hair. Consternation broke out round the meadow again. 'You *are* a foolish girl! Someone took that cat away. We can't kill him at all!'

For a moment, Gwendolen looked very dashed. Then an idea struck her. 'If I go away again, you can use my replacem—'

The watch-chains round Chrestomanci chinked. 'Nostrum, you're upsetting yourself needlessly. It was I who had the cat-violin removed. The creature's around in the garden somewhere.'

Henry Nostrum swung round to look at Chrestomanci suspiciously, still hanging on to his two wings of hair as if that kept his mind in place. 'I doubt you, sir, very seriously. You are known to be a very wily person.'

'You flatter me,' said Chrestomanci. 'Unfortunately I can't speak anything but the truth tied up in silver like this.'

Henry Nostrum looked at his brother. 'That is correct,' William said, dubiously. 'Silver constrains him to utter facts. Then I suppose the boy's missing life must be here somewhere.'

This was enough for Gwendolen, the Willing Warlock and for most of the witches and necromancers. Gwendolen said, 'I'll go and find it then,' and minced up the meadow towards the trees as fast as she could in her pointed shoes, with the Willing Warlock bouncing ahead. As they pushed past a witch in a high green hat, the witch said, 'That's right, dear. We must all hunt for the pussy.' She turned to the crowd with a witch's piercing scream. 'Hunt for pussy, everyone!'

And everyone raced off to do it, picking up skirts and holding on Sunday hats. The meadow emptied. The trees round it shook and waved and crashed. But the garden would not let anyone get very far. Brightly coloured witches, cloaked wizards and dark warlocks kept being spilt out of the trees into the meadow again. Cat heard Chrestomanci say, 'Your friends seem very ignorant, Nostrum. The way out is widdershins. Perhaps you should tell them so. The cat will certainly be in summer or spring.'

William Nostrum gave him a swirling glare and hurried off shouting, 'Widdershins, brothers and sisters! Widdershins!'

'Let me tell you, sir,' Henry Nostrum said to Chrestomanci, 'you are beginning to annoy me considerably.' He hovered for a second, but, as quite a crowd of people, with Gwendolen and the Willing Warlock among them, were whirled out of the trees into the meadow again, and seemed very indignant about it, Henry Nostrum set off trotting towards them, calling, 'No, my dear friends! My dear pupil! Widdershins. You have to go widdershins.'

Cat and Chrestomanci were left alone for the time being by the broken arch and the apple tree.

CHAPTER SIXTEEN

'Cat,' said Chrestomanci, from almost behind Cat's head. 'Cat!'

Cat did not want to talk. He was lying looking up at the blue sky through the leaves of the apple tree. Every so often it went blurred. Then Cat shut his eyes and tears ran out across both his ears. Now he knew how little Gwendolen cared about him, he was not sure he wanted any lives at all. He listened to the shouting and crashing among the trees and almost wished Fiddle would be caught soon. From time to time, he had an odd feeling that he was Fiddle himself—Fiddle furious and frightened, lashing out and scratching a huge fat witch in a flower hat.

'Cat,' said Chrestomanci. He sounded almost as desperate as Fiddle. 'Cat, I know how you're feeling. We hoped you wouldn't find out about Gwendolen for years yet. But you *are* an enchanter. I suspect that you're a stronger enchanter than I am when you set your mind to it.

Could you use some of your magic now, before someone catches poor Fiddle? Please. As a great favour. Just to help me get out of this wretched silver, so that I can summon the rest of my power.'

Cat was being Fiddle again while Chrestomanci talked. He climbed a tree, but the Willing Warlock and the Accredited Witch shook him out of it. He ran and he ran, and then jumped from between the Willing Warlock's grabbing hands, a huge jump, from somewhere immensely high. It was such a sickening jump that Cat opened his eyes. The apple leaves fluttered against the sky. The apple he could see was nearly ripe.

'What do you want me to do?' he said. 'I don't know how to do anything.'

'I know,' said Chrestomanci. 'I felt the same when they told me. Can you move your left hand at all?'

'Backwards and forwards,' Cat said, trying. 'I can't get it out of the rope though.'

'No need,' said Chrestomanci. 'You've more ability in the little finger of that hand than most people—including

Gwendolen—have in their entire lives. And the magic of the garden should help you. Just saw at the rope with your left hand and presume that the rope is made of silver.'

Cat tipped his head back and looked at Chrestomanci unbelievingly. Chrestomanci was untidy and pale and very much in earnest. He must be telling the truth. Cat moved his left hand against the rope. It felt rough and ropish. He told himself it was not rough rope, it was silver. And the rope felt smooth. But sawing was rather a strain. Cat lifted his hand as far as he could get it and brought the edge of it down on the silver rope.

Clink. Jingle. The rope parted.

'Thank you,' said Chrestomanci. 'There go two watch-chains. But there seems to be a very firm spell on these handcuffs. Can you try again?'

The rope was a great deal looser. Cat fought his way out of it with a series of clatters and thumps—he was not sure quite what he had turned it into—and knelt up on the stone. Chrestomanci walked weakly towards him, with his hands still hanging limply in the handcuffs. At the same time, the Willing Warlock spilt out of the trees, arguing with the witch in the flower hat.

'I tell you the cat's dead. It fell a good fifty feet.'

'But I tell you they always fall on their feet.'

'Then why didn't it get up then?'

Cat realised there was no time to waste trying to imagine things. He put both hands to the handcuffs and wrenched.

'Ow!' said Chrestomanci.

But the handcuffs were off. Cat was suddenly very pleased with his new-found talent. He broke the handcuffs in two and told them to be ferocious eagles. 'Get after the Nostrums,' he said. The left handcuff took off savagely as ordered, but the right half was still a silver handcuff and it fell on the grass. Cat had to pick it up in his left hand before it would do as it was told.

Cat looked round then to see what Chrestomanci was doing. He was standing under the apple tree, and the talkative little man called Bernard was stumbling down the hillside toward him.

Bernard's Sunday cravat was comfortably undone. He was carrying a pencil and a newspaper folded open at the crossword. 'Enchantment, five letters, ending in C,' he was murmuring, before he looked up and saw Chrestomanci green with tree-mould. He stared at the two watch-chains, Cat, the rope, and the numbers of people who were hurrying among the trees round the top of the meadow. 'Bless my soul!' he said. 'I'm sorry—I had no idea I was needed. You need the others too?'

'Rather quickly,' said Chrestomanci.

The witch in the flower hat saw him standing away from the tree and raised her voice in a witch's scream. 'They're getting away! Stop them!'

Witches, warlocks, necromancers and wizards poured out into the meadow, with Gwendolen mincing among them, and hurriedly cast spells as they came. Muttering rolled round the garden. The smell of magic grew thick. Chrestomanci held up one hand as if he was asking for silence. The muttering grew instead, and sounded angry. But none of the people muttering came any nearer. The only ones who were still moving were William and Henry Nostrum, who kept spilling out from the trees, running hard and bawling faintly, each with a large flapping eagle after him.

Bernard chewed his pencil and his face looked ribby. 'This is awful! There are so many of them!'

'Keep trying. I'm giving you all the help I can spare,' Chrestomanci said, with an anxious look at the muttering crowd.

Bernard's bushy eyebrows bobbed up. 'Ah!'

Miss Bessemer was standing above him on the slope. She had the works of a clock in one hand and a cloth in the other. Perhaps because of the slope, she seemed taller and more purple of dress than usual. She took in the situation at a glance. 'You'll need a full muster to deal with this lot,' she said to Chrestomanci.

A witch in the muttering crowd screamed, 'He's getting help!' Cat thought it was Gwendolen. The smell of magic grew, and the muttering became like a long roll of thunder. The crowd seemed to be edging forward slowly, in a bobbing of fancy hats and a bristle of dark suits. The hand Chrestomanci was holding up to stop them began to shake.

'The garden's helping them, too,' said Bernard. 'Put forth your best, Bessie-girl.' He chewed his pencil and frowned intensely. Miss Bessemer wrapped her cloth neatly round her pieces of clock and grew noticeably taller.

And suddenly the rest of the Family began to appear round the apple tree, all in the middle of the peaceful Sunday things they had been doing when they were summoned. One of the younger ladies had a skein of wool between her hands, and one of the younger men was winding it. The next man was holding a billiard cue, and the other young lady had a lump of chalk. The old lady with mittens was crocheting a new pair of mittens. Mr Saunders appeared with a thump. He had the dragon tucked playfully under one arm, and both of them looked startled to be fetched in the middle of a romp.

The dragon saw Cat. It wriggled out from under Mr Saunders's arm, bounded across the grass, and jumped

326

rattling and flaming into Cat's arms. Cat found himself staggering about under the apple tree with quite a heavy dragon squirming on his chest and enthusiastically licking his face with flame. It would have burnt him badly if he had not remembered in time to tell the flames they were cool.

He looked up to see Roger and Julia appearing. They both had their arms stretched stiffly above their heads, because they had been playing mirrors again, and they were both very much astonished. 'It's the garden!' said Roger. 'And loads of people!'

'You never summoned us before, Daddy,' said Julia.

'This is rather special,' said Chrestomanci. He was holding his right hand up with his left one by now, and looking tired out. 'I need you to fetch your mother. Quickly.'

'We're holding them,' Mr Saunders said. He was trying to sound encouraging, but he was nervous. The muttering crowd was coming nearer.

'No, we aren't!' snapped the old lady in mittens. 'We can't do anything more without Milly.'

Cat had a feeling that everyone was trying to fetch Milly. He thought he ought to help, since they needed her so much, but he did not know what to do. Besides, the dragon's flames were so hot that he needed all his energy not to get burnt.

Roger and Julia could not fetch Milly. 'What's wrong?' said Julia. 'We've always been able to before.'

'All these people's spells are stopping us,' said Roger.

'Try again,' said Chrestomanci. 'I can't. Something's stopping me, too.'

'Are you joining in the magic?' the dragon asked Cat. Cat was finding the heat of it really troublesome by now. His face was red and sore. But, as soon as the dragon spoke, he understood. He *was* joining in the magic. Only he was joining in on the wrong side, because Gwendolen was using him again. He was so used to her doing it that he barely noticed. But he could feel her doing it now. She was using so much of his power to stop Chrestomanci fetching Milly, that Cat was getting burnt.

For the first time in his life, Cat was angry about it. 'She's no business to!' he told the dragon. And he took his magic back. It was like a cool draught in his face.

'Cat! Stop that!' Gwendolen screamed from the crowd

'Oh shut up!' Cat shouted back. 'It's mine!'

At his feet, the little spring ran bubbling out of the grass again. Cat was looking down at it, wondering why it should, when he noticed a sort of gladness come over the anxious Family around him. Chrestomanci was looking upwards, and a light seemed to have fallen across his face. Cat turned round and found Milly was there at last. He supposed it was some trick of the hillside that made her look tall as the apple tree. But it seemed no trick that she also looked kind at the end of a long day. She had Fiddle in her arms. Fiddle was draggled and miserable, but purring.

'I'm so sorry,' Milly said. 'I'd have come sooner if I'd known. This poor beast had fallen off the garden wall and I wasn't thinking of anything else.'

Chrestomanci smiled, and let his hand go. He did not seem to need it to hold back the crowd any more. They stood where they were, and their muttering had stopped. 'It doesn't matter,' he said. 'But we must get to work now.'

The Family got to work at once. Cat found it hard to describe or remember afterwards just how they did. He remembered claps and peals of thunder, darkness and mist. He thought Chrestomanci grew taller than Milly, tall as the sky—but that could have been because the dragon got extremely scared and Cat was kneeling in the grass to make it feel safer. From there he saw the Family from time to time, striding about like giants. Witches screamed and screamed. Warlocks and wizards roared and howled. Sometimes there was whirling white rain, whirling white snow, or perhaps just whirling white smoke, whirling and whirling. Cat was sure the whole garden was spinning, faster and faster. Among the whirling and the whiteness came flying necromancers, or Bernard striding, or Mr Saunders, billowing, with snow in his hair. Julia ran past, making knot after knot in her handkerchief. And Milly must have brought reinforcements with her. Cat glimpsed Euphemia, the butler, a footman, two gardeners and, to his alarm, Will Suggins once, breasting the whiteness in the howling, spinning, screaming garden.

The spinning got so fast that Cat was no longer giddy. It was spinning rocksteady, and humming. Chrestomanci stepped out of the whiteness and under the apple tree and held out one hand to Cat. He was wet and windswept, and Cat was still not sure how tall he was. 'Can I have some of your dragon's blood?' Chrestomanci said.

'How did you know I'd got it?' Cat said guiltily, letting go of the dragon in order to get at his crucible.

'The smell,' said Chrestomanci.

Cat passed his crucible over. 'Here you are. Have I lost a life over it?'

'Not you,' said Chrestomanci. 'But it was lucky you didn't let Janet touch it.' He stepped to the whirling, and emptied the whole crucible into it. Cat saw the powder snatched away and whirled. The mist turned brownish red and the humming to a terrible bell-note that hurt Cat's ears. He could hear witches and warlocks howling with horror. 'Let them roar,' said Chrestomanci. He was leaning against the right-hand pillar of the archway. 'Every single one of them has now lost his or her witchcraft. They'll complain to their MPs and there'll be questions asked in Parliament, but I daresay we shall survive it.' He raised his hand and beckoned.

Frantic people in soaking wet Sunday clothes came whirling out of the whiteness and were sucked through the broken arch like dead leaves in a whirlpool. More and more and more came. They sailed through in crowds. Out of the whirling many, Chrestomanci somehow collected the two Nostrums and put them down for a minute in front of Cat and the dragon. Cat was charmed to see one of his eagles sitting on Henry Nostrum's shoulders, pecking at his bald place, and the other eagle fluttering round William stabbing at the stouter parts of him.

'Call them off,' said Chrestomanci.

Cat called them off, rather regretfully, and they fell on the grass as handcuffs. Then the handcuffs were swept away with the Nostrum brothers and whirled through the archway with them in the last of the crowd.

Last of all came Gwendolen. Chrestomanci stopped her, too. As he did so, the whiteness cleared, the humming died away and the rest of the Family began to collect on the sunny hillside, panting a little but not very wet. Cat thought the garden was probably still spinning. But perhaps it always did. Gwendolen stared round in horror.

'Let me go! I've got to go back and be queen.'

'Don't be so selfish,' said Chrestomanci. 'You've no right to keep snatching eight other people from world to world. Stay here and learn how to do it properly. And those courtiers of yours don't really do what you say, you know. They only pretend.'

'I don't care!' Gwendolen screamed. She held up her golden clothes, kicked off her pointed shoes, and ran for the archway. Chrestomanci reached out to stop her. Gwendolen spun round and hurled her last handful of dragon's blood in his face and while Chrestomanci was forced to duck and put one arm over his face, Gwendolen backed hastily through the archway. There was a mighty bang. The space between the pillars turned black. When everyone recovered, Gwendolen was gone. There was nothing but meadow between the pillars again. Even the pointed shoes had gone.

'What did the child do?' said the old lady with mittens, very shaken.

'Sealed herself in that world,' said Chrestomanci. He was even more shaken. 'Isn't that so, Cat?' he said.

Cat nodded mulishly. It had seemed worth it. He was not sure he wanted to see Gwendolen again.

'And look what that's done,' said Mr Saunders, nodding at the hillside.

Janet was stumbling down the slope, past Milly, and she was crying. Milly handed Fiddle carefully to Julia and put her arms round Janet. Janet sobbed heavily. The rest crowded round her. Bernard patted Janet's back and the old lady with mittens made soothing noises.

Cat stood on his own near the ruins, with the dragon looking enquiringly up at him from the grass. Janet had been happy in her own world. She had missed her mother and father. Now she was probably in this world for good, and Cat had done it. And Chrestomanci had called Gwendolen selfish!

'No, it's not that, quite, really,' Janet said from the midst of the Family. She tried to sit down on the fallen block of stone, and got up quickly, remembering the way it was being used when she last saw it.

Cat had a very gallant idea. He sent for a blue velvet chair from Gwendolen's room and put it down on the grass beside Janet. Janet gave a tearful laugh. 'That was kind.' She started to sit in it.

'I belong to Chrestomanci Castle,' said the chair. 'I belong to Chresto—' Miss Bessemer looked at it sternly and it stopped.

Janet sat in the chair. It was a little wobbly because the grass was uneven. 'Where's Cat?' she said anxiously.

'I'm here,' said Cat. 'I got the chair for

you.' He thought it was kind of Janet to look so relieved to see him.

'What do you say to a little lunch?' Milly asked Miss Bessemer. 'It must be nearly two o'clock.'

'Agreed,' said Miss Bessemer, and made a stately half-turn towards the butler. He nodded. The footman and the gardeners staggered forward with great hampers like laundry baskets, which, when the lids were thrown back, proved to be full of chickens, hams, meat-pies, jellies, fruit and wine.

'Oh, beautiful!' said Roger.

Everyone sat round to eat the lunch. Most of them sat on the grass, and Cat made sure to sit as far away from Will Suggins as he could. Milly sat on the stone slab. Chrestomanci splashed some of the water from the bubbling spring over his face—which seemed to refresh him wonderfully—and sat leaning against the slab. The old lady with mittens produced a tuffet out of nowhere, which she said was more comfortable; and Bernard thoughtfully shook out the remains of the rope that Cat had left by the rock. It became a hammock. Bernard strung it between the pillars of the archway and lay in it, looking defiantly comfortable, even though he had the greatest difficulty keeping his balance and eating as well. Fiddle was given a wing of chicken and took it into the apple tree to eat, out of the way of the dragon. The dragon was jealous of Fiddle. It divided its time between breathing resentful smoke up into the tree and leaning heavily against Cat, begging for chicken and meat-pie.

'I warn you,' said Mr Saunders. 'That is the most spoilt dragon in the world.'

'I'm the *only* dragon in the world,' the dragon said smugly.

Janet was still inclined to be tearful. 'My dear, we do understand,' said Milly, 'and we're so very sorry.'

'I can send you back,' said Chrestomanci. 'It's not quite so easy with Gwendolen's world missing from the series, but don't think it can't be done.'

'No, no. That's all right,' Janet gulped. 'At least, it will be all right when I'm used to it. I was hoping to come back here—but it is rather a wrench. You

337

see—' Her eyes filled and her mouth trembled. A handkerchief came out of the air and pushed itself into her hand. Cat did not know who had done it, but he wished he had thought of it. 'Thanks,' said Janet. 'You see, Mum and Dad haven't noticed the difference.' She blew her nose furiously. 'I got back to my bedroom, and the other girl—she's called Romillia really—had been writing her diary. She got called away in mid-sentence and left it lying there, so I read it. And it was all about how scared she had been in case my parents noticed she wasn't me, and how glad she was when she was clever enough to make sure they didn't. She was utterly terrified of being sent back. She'd had a dreadful life as an orphan in her own world, and she was miserable there. She'd written things that made me feel really sorry for her. Mind you,' Janet said severely, 'she was just asking for trouble keeping a diary in the same house as my parents. I wrote a note in it telling her so, and I said if she *must* keep one, she'd better put it in one of my good hiding places. And then—and then I sat

338

there and rather hoped I'd come back.'

'That was kind of you,' said Cat.

'It was, and you're truly welcome, my love,' said Milly.

'You're sure?' Chrestomanci asked, looking searchingly at Janet over the chicken leg he was eating.

Janet nodded, quite firmly, though most of her face was still hidden in the handkerchief.

'You were the one I was most worried about,' Chrestomanci said. 'I'm afraid I didn't realise at once what had happened. Gwendolen had found out about the mirror, you see, and she worked the change in her bathroom. And anyway, none of us had the slightest idea Cat's powers were that strong. The truth only dawned on me during that unfortunate affair of the frog, and then of course I took a look at once to see what had happened to Gwendolen and the seven other girls. Gwendolen was in her element. And Jennifer, who came after Romillia, is as tough as Gwendolen and has always wished she was an orphan; whereas Queen Caroline, whom Gwendolen displaced, was as miserable as Romillia, and had run away three times already. And it was the same with the other five. They were all much better suited—except perhaps you.'

Janet took her face out of the handkerchief and looked at him in large indignation. 'Why couldn't you have *told* me you knew? I wouldn't have been nearly so scared of you! And you wouldn't believe the troubles Cat got into because of it—not to speak of me owing Mr Bagwash twenty pounds and not knowing the Geography and History here! And you needn't laugh!' she said, as nearly everyone did.

'I apologise,' said Chrestomanci. 'Believe me, it was one of the most troubling decisions I've ever had to make. But who on earth is Mr Bagwash?'

'Mr Baslam,' Cat explained reluctantly. 'Gwendolen bought some dragon's blood from him and didn't really pay.'

'He's asking outrageously much,' said Milly. 'And it is illegal, you know.'

'I'll go and have a word with him tomorrow,' Bernard said from his hammock. 'Though he'll probably be gone by then. He knows I've got my eye on him.'

'Why was it a troubling decision?' Janet asked Chrestomanci.

Chrestomanci tossed his chicken bone to the dragon and slowly wiped his fingers on a handkerchief with a gold-embroidered C in one corner. This gave him an excuse to turn Cat's way and stare, in his vaguest way, into the air above Cat's head. Since Cat was fairly clear by now that the vaguer Chrestomanci seemed about something, the more acutely he was attending to it, he was not altogether surprised when Chrestomanci said, 'Because of Cat. We would have felt a good deal easier if Cat could have brought himself to tell someone what had happened. We gave him a number of opportunities to. But when he held his tongue, we thought perhaps he did know the extent of his powers after all.'

'But I don't,' said Cat. And Janet, who was becoming thoroughly cheerful now she was being allowed to ask questions, said, 'I think you were quite wrong. We both got so frightened that we came into this garden and nearly got you and Cat killed. You should have said.'

'Perhaps,' agreed Chrestomanci, and peeled a banana in a thoughtful way. He was still turned towards Cat. 'Normally we're more than a match here for people like the Nostrums. I knew they were planning something through Gwendolen, and I thought Cat knew it too—my apologies, Cat. I wouldn't have had Gwendolen here for a minute, except that we had to have Cat. Chrestomanci *has* to be a nine-lifed enchanter. No one else is strong enough for the post.'

'Post?' said Janet. 'Isn't it a hereditary title then?' Mr Saunders laughed, and threw his bone to the dragon, too. 'Heavens no! We're all Government employees here. The job Chrestomanci has is to make sure this world isn't run entirely by witches. Ordinary people have rights too. And he has to make sure witches don't get out into worlds where there isn't so much magic and play havoc there. It's a big job. And we're the staff that helps him.'

'And he needs us like he needs two left legs,' Bernard remarked, jerking about in the hammock as he tried to eat a jelly.

'Oh, come now!' said Chrestomanci. 'I'd have been sunk without you today.'

'I was thinking of the way you found the next Chrestomanci,' Bernard said, spooning jelly off his waistcoat. 'You did it, when we were just going round in circles.'

'Nine-lifed enchanters are not easy to find,' Chrestomanci explained to Janet. 'In the first place, they're very rare, and in the second, they have to use their magic before they can be found. And Cat didn't. We were actually thinking of bringing someone in from another world, when Cat happened to fall into the hands of a clairvoyant. Even then, we only knew where he was, not who. I'd no idea he was Eric Chant, or any relation of mine at all—though I suppose I might have remembered that his parents were cousins, which doubled the chance of their children being witches. And I must confess that Frank Chant wrote to me to say his daughter was a witch and seemed to be using her younger brother in some way. Forgive me, Cat. I ignored that letter, because your father had been so very rude when I offered to make sure his children would be born without witchcraft.'

'Just as well he was rude, you know,' Bernard said.

'Was that what the letters were about?' said Cat.

'I don't understand,' said Janet, 'why you didn't say anything at all to Cat. Why couldn't you?'

Chrestomanci was still looking vaguely in Cat's direction. Cat could tell he was very wary indeed. 'Like this,' he said. 'Remember we hadn't known one another very long. Cat appears to have no magic at all. Yet his sister works magic far beyond her own abilities, and goes on doing it even when her witchcraft is taken away. What am I to think? Does Cat know what he's doing? If he doesn't, why doesn't he? And if he does know, what is he up to? When Gwendolen removed herself, and nobody mentioned the fact, I hoped some of the answers might emerge. And

Cat still does nothing—'

'What do you mean, nothing?' said Janet. 'There were some fabulous conkers, and he kept stopping Julia.'

'Yes, and I couldn't think what was happening,' Julia said, rather shamed.

Cat felt hurt and uncomfortable. 'Leave me alone!' he said, and he stood up. Everyone, even Chrestomanci, went tense. The only person who did not was Janet, and Cat could hardly count her, because she was not used to magic. He found he was trying not to cry, which made him very much ashamed. 'Stop treating me so carefully!' he said. 'I'm not a fool, or a baby. You're all afraid of me, aren't you? You didn't tell me things and you didn't punish Gwendolen because you were afraid I'd do something dreadful. And I haven't. I don't know how to. I didn't know I could.'

'My love, it was just that no one was sure,' said Milly.

'Well, be sure now!' said Cat. 'The only things I did were by mistake, like coming here in this garden—and turning Euphemia into a frog, I suppose, but I didn't know it was me.'

'You're not to worry about that, Eric,' said Euphemia from the hillside, where she was sitting with Will Suggins. 'It was the shock upset me. I know enchanters are different from us witches. And I'll speak to Mary. I promise.'

'Speak to Will Suggins too, while you're at it,' said Janet. 'Because he's going to turn Cat into a frog in revenge any minute now.'

Euphemia bounced round on the hillside to look at Will. 'What?' she said.

'What is this, Will?' Chrestomanci asked.

'I laid it on him—for three o'clock, sir,' Will Suggins said apprehensively, 'if he didn't meet me as a tiger.'

Chrestomanci took out a large gold watch. 'Hm. It's about due now. If you don't mind my saying so, that was a little foolish of you, Will. Suppose you carry on. Turn Cat into a frog, or yourself into a tiger, or both. I shan't interfere.'

Will Suggins climbed heavily to his feet and stood facing Cat, looking as if he would prefer to be several miles away. 'Let the dough work, then,' he said.

Cat was still feeling so upset and tearful that he wondered whether to oblige Will Suggins and become a frog. Or he could try being a flea instead. But it all seemed rather silly. 'Why don't you be a tiger?' he said.

As Cat expected, Will Suggins made a beautiful tiger, long-backed and sleek and sharply striped. He was heavy as he padded up and down the slope, but his legs slid so easily in the silky folds of his hide that he almost seemed light. But Will Suggins himself spoilt the effect by rubbing a distressed paw over his huge cat face and staring appealingly at Chrestomanci. Chrestomanci simply laughed. The dragon trotted up the hill to investigate this new beast. Will Suggins was so alarmed that he reared up on his great hind legs to get away from it. It looked so ungainly for a tiger to be doing that, that Cat turned him back to Will Suggins on the spot.

'It wasn't real?' asked the dragon.

'No!' said Will Suggins, mopping his face with his sleeve. 'All right, lad, you win. How did you do it so quick?'

'I don't know,' Cat said

apologetically. 'I've really no idea. Shall I learn when you teach me magic?' he asked Mr Saunders.

Mr Saunders looked a little blank. 'Well—'

'No, Michael,' said Chrestomanci, 'is the right answer. It's quite clear elementary magic isn't going to mean much to Cat. I'll have to teach you myself, Cat, and we'll be starting on Advanced Theory, I think, by the look of it. You seem to start where most people leave off.'

'But why didn't he know?' Janet demanded. 'It always makes me angry not to know things, and I feel specially angry about this, because it seems so hard on Cat.'

'It is, I agree,' said Chrestomanci. 'But it's something in the nature of enchanters' magic, I think. Something the same happened to me. I couldn't do magic either. I couldn't do anything. But they found I had nine lives—I lost them at such a rate that it soon became obvious—and they told me I had to be the next Chrestomanci when I grew up, which absolutely appalled me, because I couldn't work the simplest spell. So they sent me to a tutor, the most terrifying old person, who was supposed to find what the trouble was. And he took one look at me and snarled, "Empty your pockets, Chant!" Which I did. I was too scared not to. I took out my silver watch, and one and sixpence, and a silver charm from my godmother, and a silver tiepin I had forgotten to wear, and a silver brace I was supposed to wear in my teeth. And as soon as they were gone, I did some truly startling things. As I remember, the roof of the tutor's house came off.'

'Is it really true about silver then?' Janet said.

'For me, yes,' said Chrestomanci.

'Yes, poor darling,' Milly said, smiling at him. 'It's so awkward with money. He can only handle pound notes and coppers.'

'He has to give us our pocket-money in pennies, if Michael hasn't got it,' said Roger. 'Imagine sixty pennies in your pocket.'

'The really difficult thing is mealtimes,' said Milly. 'He can't do a thing with a knife and fork in his hands—and Gwendolen would do awful things during dinner.'

'How stupid!' said Janet. 'Why on earth don't you use stainless steel cutlery?'

Milly and Chrestomanci looked at one another. 'I never thought of it!' said Milly. 'Janet, my love, it's a very good thing you're staying here!'

Janet looked at Cat and laughed. And Cat, though he was still a little lonely and tearful, managed to laugh too.

Photoset, printed and bound in Great Britain by REDWOOD BURN LIMITED, Trowbridge, Wiltshire